Candy in Action

Candy in Action

* by *

Matthue Roth

Soft Skull Press
* Brooklyn, NY *
** 2008 **

bs"d

Candy In Action
© 2008 Matthue Roth

ISBN: 1-933368-63-2
ISBN-13: 978-1-933368-63-4

Published by Soft Skull Press
55 Washington St., Suite 804
Brooklyn, NY 11201
www.softskull.com

Cover Design by David Barnett
Cover Art by David Barnett and Jaime Rose Mendola
Interior Design by Anne Horowitz

Distributed by Publishers Group West
www.pgw.com 1-800-788-3123

Printed in the United States of America

Library of Congress Cataloging-in-Publication Data

Chapters

What I Got

(prologue)

Life has rules. The Law of Gravity. The Rules of Motion. The most popular girl has to date the captain of the football team. It's all pretty logical and generally accepted stuff.

And people on the street definitely aren't supposed to turn into crazy, semiautomatic-wielding maniacs . . .

But life has its own plans for me. That much, I've known for a while.

Then one day it was like, suddenly the world turned completely upside down, and I was the only one who still remembered which way was up.

*
* *

I was born outside Atlanta, which, eighteen years later, was where I still lived. My mom, besides being the consummate society wife, was a total control freak. I mean, in retrospect, she may have had an actual obsessive-compulsive disorder, but as a kid, I just thought she was crazy. In sixth grade, when all the other girls were waking up two hours before school to put on their makeup, my mom was waking me three hours early to put on mine. I dutifully painted my face and then slipped on my huge glasses and hid all the delicate face artistry beneath.

That wasn't usually a problem or anything, though, because I was kept too busy to be delicate. As my father watched, too afraid to put a name to her mania, my mom enrolled me in ballet, piano, violin, private cooking classes, tennis, golf, swimming, and kung fu. She was careful never to get too proud of me.

Instead, she pushed harder.

She died when I was in seventh grade. That same year, my life changed—totally unrelatedly—in the most unexpected way of all.

I got contact lenses.

That day, in the doctor's office, he showed me how to handle my contacts and to hold my eyelids open while I dropped the tiny plastic satellite-dishes in. On the way back out, I accidentally left my bulky old glasses sitting on the table in the waiting room.

The secretary ran after me, clutching those glasses. "Don't you want these?" she called to me, as I was already crossing the street.

When I turned around and flashed her a sassy glare—the look that had, so far, not attracted any unruly attention from anyone—the secretary, who was a fiery-looking woman in her own right, blushed and cleared her throat, whispering a quiet, "never mind."

And suddenly, I went from working-at-it popular to being top-shelf beautiful.

I'm not saying this to brag. I was beautiful. It hit me, the same way that you suddenly realize where steak comes from, that I was now stunning. I could only tell by the way people stared at me. Everyone, whether they knew me or not, stared at me, obviously and lustfully—either like I was edible, or like they were afraid of breaking me.

And, just like that, I became the most popular girl in school.

I got straight As without trying. I got dates without asking.

I would have dated the captain of the football team, too, except he was gay. In tenth grade, we went to soph hop together, and he kept trying to hook up with me like crazy and I kept swatting him away, and at the end of the night, after all the after parties and photo ops, we were alone in his car and he was like, "Actually, it's okay, I don't like girls anyway."

The night was absolutely perfect after that.

But you know what? That's kind of how my life went. I loved being top-shelf popular, but it also kind of sucked. Nobody talks to you. Everyone's afraid that, I don't know, they're going to get stared at just as much as everyone stares at you. They're afraid that your popularity is going to rub off on them, and then they'll lose control of their lives as much as you've already lost control of yours.

*

*   *

Look, I'm not going to lie. This is a story about some really beautiful people who do some really screwed-up things. People die. Sometimes the wrong people die, and sometimes the right people kill them. Things get really bad, and they don't always get better again. That's what I learned.

But some things do get better.

And I'm gonna be one of them.

Holiday

(1)

"Hey, Candy. You want to go to Spain today?"

"Velma, you are a *monster*," I groaned, pulling the phone away from my ear. I looked at the clock. Flaming red numbers burned themselves into my eyes. "It's eight o'clock in the morning."

"And in Spain, it's already two P.M.," said Velma. "Are you in or not? Inquiring minds want to know, honey."

"I want to sleep."

"You won't be able to fall back. You never can."

Velma and I had been friends since birth. She knew how to manage me the way cabbies in New York manage traffic. From anyone else, I wouldn't tolerate that kind of behavior for a second—I'd walk out the door, screen their phone calls, and never look them in the eye again.

But Velma was my best friend. We'd made it through hurricanes, junior high cafeteria food, and a stream of guys a hundred miles long. She was the only one who could treat me this way, and she knew it.

I checked the clock again. I glared at the numbers like it was the clock's fault.

"Make sure I'm back in time for classes tomorrow?"

I managed to say between grunts.

"Deal," Velma agreed chirpily.

"Okay," I said into the phone. "But I'm not packing."

Velma's car service picked me up thirty minutes later. By then, I'd showered, stuffed a daypack (eyeliner, blush, passport, and my Italian phrasebook—the closest to Spanish that I could find), and changed into a tsubi denim miniskirt and a rainbow bikini top.

The rear window rolled down, and Velma's head popped out. "That's what you're wearing to Spain?" she said.

I shrugged. "I told you, I am *not* planning on staying overnight."

"All we'll *have* is overnight, at this rate," Velma grumbled.

I cracked her door open. She slid down the long leather bench and I eased in.

No matter how often we hung out, it was still funny to see Velma order people around. Barely five feet tall, with a high, squeaky voice and moppy blond hair, Velma still looked basically like a kid. I mean, she'd matured, but while I hit a growth spurt—I was five foot ten now, taller than my last three boyfriends—Velma had this eternally child-lit presence, bouncy and grabby and curious as hell. She was also one of the richest eighteen-year-olds in the country, so to watch her throw money around, seemingly without a care in the world, enforced that jejune, not-a-care-in-the-world image that she didn't even *try* to get past.

"So, why Spain?" I asked, once she'd bought us tickets and we'd gotten past security ("Oh, Ms. Knight, Ms. Cohen. Where to today?") and we were sitting comfortably on the plane. Velma had managed to secure us the last seats on a plane that was supposed to leave as soon as we pulled up to the airport, and they hustled us into first class as the flight attendants were wrapping safety belts around themselves in the aisles. The flight attendant who escorted us recognized Velma.

His eyes twinkled knowingly as he brushed us past the cabin crew. I swear—I know we all lead charmed lives, but Velma's is positively a miracle.

She turned from the window to me, that same innocently curious look. "Oh, I don't know—Christopher was thinking of cooking Spanish food for me tomorrow, and I couldn't tell him it tasted authentic if I didn't *know*, could I?"

I rolled my eyes. "Velms, are you still *with* him?"

Velma looked uncomfortable. "I don't know."

"How can you not know?"

"If you ask *him*, I am."

Velma wasn't fat, but she was definitely kind of round, what her grandmother liked to call *pleasantly plump*. And she totally made up for it with how cute she was. She was so short and pristine, she looked like a porcelain doll. I was always skinny as a rail, and tall, too. Next to her, I looked like RuPaul or something, absolutely towering over her. I'm sure it gave Velma a complex.

That lasted up until sometime last year. I don't know if it was the sudden rush of realizing how temporary our lives were, when we were about to move out and go to college and become adults, or maybe just that thing that happens to girls when we notice guys noticing us and, suddenly, we realize how much power we could have. For Velma, it took a lot longer. But, when she blossomed, she *blossomed*—and soon, my Saturday night safety date had dates of her own. Velma would double- and triple-book herself into reams of trouble, and then she would abruptly cancel, based on what kind of mood she was in. And all of this would've been fine, if only she didn't feel so damn *guilty* about it.

That was why these little runaway vacations were good for her. Like unplugging your computer so you lose all your homework.

Sometimes, you just have to start over.

*

*   *

We landed in Madrid early in the evening. The streets were just beginning to sparkle, revving up for the night. Velma ordered a car that drove us to our hotel, and as it poured through the dusty boulevards, cool night air swept in through the slits between window and door. Velma stared out, taking in the city. She was so in charge.

"What should we do first, Candy?" Velma asked, as we entered the hotel. "We can stop in a bar and have margaritas or go to a restaurant. Or we can check out the clubs."

"Mm," I said absently. I was trying not to think about the ginormous expenses that we were both incurring upon Velma's family. Just *breathing* in this hotel probably cost more than I made in a month. It was no problem, of course—my family was well-off, and Velma's grand-parents had enough money to make us look destitute. Tonight, I just felt like riding the waves of fate.

The lobby had *trompe l'oeil* ceilings and pastel murals on the walls. I made Velma wait while I dropped our bags in the room, and when I came back (with flowers in hand—*"Todo mon amor, Christopher"*), I found Velma sitting on a couch, talking with a certain recording artist who sometimes hung out with us back in Atlanta.

As discreetly as I could, I swept the flowers behind my back, knowing full well it was next to impossible to hide such a huge bouquet—especially in a bikini top that barely hid *me*—but making the effort, anyway.

I smiled graciously.

"Candy, baby," he said. On his albums he had the gruffest hip-hop voice. In person, it was soft and kind of musical. He opened his arms like he expected me to fall into them. "You gonna give me some love or what?"

"What kind of a way is that to ask, babe?" I knew he thought saying *babe* was flirty. Really, it was just to remind him who was in charge.

"Aw, you called me *babe*. That's good enough."

"Baby"—the corners of my mouth twitched—"call me a skeptic, but I don't remember the last time *anything* was enough for you."

"Candy, girl, you know me entirely too well. Now, give poppa some sugar, won't ya?"

I walked over, hugged him in the lightest and briefest way possible, and stepped away. I hated it when guys were like that—asking for a hug, like you wouldn't give it to them if they didn't. I mean, *I* probably wouldn't, but that's just the kind of girl I am. Part of that post-glasses period of my life was learning how to be subtle and sublime.

I liked being subtle. I really did. It made everyone else think I was mysterious, and I got to spend more time inside my own thoughts, instead of blabbing them all out to the world and sounding like an airhead.

"Damn, Candy," he said. "You look better every time I see you."

The rap star was used to being low-key. He had a du rag pulled around his head to hide his bleach blond buzz cut, thick sunglasses, and a baggy hoodie shrouding his face. His arms were perpetually crossed, and his right hand played in front of his face when he talked. He was kind of a friend of ours. He was more Velma's friend than mine. He was a total player, and we *were* friendly, but that didn't mean that he wasn't always trying to get with me.

I smiled, but only slightly.

I realized just then that I'd been holding the bouquet of flowers incognito, kind of behind my back and kind of behind my skirt. Just then, I spotted a trash can by the sofa and poured in the flowers.

He watched them drop. "I see I'm not the first to try and pique your interest this evening," he said, cocking a smile behind his hand.

I arched one flawless eyebrow. I perfected *that* move three days after I got my contacts.

"Were there flowers in the room?" Velma sounded a little too hopeful.

I flashed her a whatever-are-you-talking-about? look.

Our rapper friend jammed his hands in his too-big jean pockets. He looked around the room, trying to look inconspicuous. Boy, was it hard.

"They were from Christopher, weren't they?" asked Velma, all suspicion and glares.

"Forget about him. The card was in Spanish, and it was *so* not even grammatically correct," I told her apologetically. "I think he looked it up online."

"Well then, let's just do a little language experimentation of our own," she said, a big smile spreading across her face. "I think it's about time to see what this country is made of."

That night, we skipped dinner and went to the clubs. No matter where we were, one of the three of us had connections at the club. If all else failed, they just looked at our friend's face and passed us to the front of the line. We poured through the clubs that night, eight of them, drinking at most, dancing at all. The bartenders loved us, and we carried the party wherever we went. We ditched our rapper after the third bar, when two college students from Barcelona with slicked-back hair and bling the color of skyscrapers ran us out through the back door and took us to their favorite dive bar. We left there, too, but not before one college guy hoisted Velma onto the pool table and necked with her furiously.

The other guy tried to get with me. I changed the subject. I asked him about couture in Barcelona.

We ran to another club, and then another, and by the sixth, Velma was definitely not feeling so afflicted with Christopher. I was wound tight and dancing, sliding from guy to guy and by myself, swinging my hips against the dance floor, and then against the sunrise, hopping from club to club, and from cab to cab, and by the time we pulled into the airport, two minutes away from missing our morning flight—"Ms. Knight, Ms. Cohen, don't worry, we've stalled the plane for you" *(ahem)* "again"—I remembered that we'd never been back to our hotel room.

"Don't worry," said Velma, flipping out her cell phone. "I'll have them mail our stuff to us."

Tuition

(2)

The restaurant that night was a total cyclone. Plates blew everywhere like shrapnel. The food cascaded down in layers from the chef's hands: roll (bottom half), burger, red onion, lettuce, tomato, mayonnaise, roll (top half), sesame seeds raining down in a delicate sprinkle.

The plate whizzed into my hand. I slipped it into position. I could carry three plates at a time, one in each hand and one in the crux of my elbow. I brought them out to tables and sent them flying down the mahogany.

This was Steaks & Co., a restaurant that tried to be a lot more upscale than it actually was, serving three-dollar burgers on nice-looking dishes for $12.95. The average customers were middle-class families celebrating birthday dinners, or men in expensive business suits, stopping on the way home from the overtime crunch at work. On a good night the plates slid into place in front of each customer like flying saucers, waiting to take over the world.

This was not a good night.

Plates collided. Stacks of plates on my arm squashed the tops of burger rolls into crop circles. Vials of ketchup spilled over, fries tumbled in an avalanche into this businessman's lap and he grumped loudly and the family behind him turned around. He was already pissed that I didn't lean over to put his food down so he could look down the front of my shirt.

Did I tell you, I was only here for fun?

"I'm sorry," I mumbled, scooping up fries with one hand, brushing a stray strand of hair out of my face with the other. It felt really important to me that he understood how I was only doing this to pay for college.

"I'm only doing this to pay for college," I said.

"Well, *that* doesn't make my food taste any better," the businessman grumbled, snatching a handful of fries from the table and stuffing them in his mouth.

He was fat and he chewed with his mouth open. I wondered whether he was married. I wondered if his wife was pretty, and if she hooked up with him because he offered her things: money, stability, the security of knowing he's so ugly and rude that he will be unable to ever find another woman to cheat on her with. Sometimes I wondered what kind of guy I was going to end up with.

But that got me thinking about bigger questions, and I shut it off immediately.

I mean, I still had four hours to go before I clocked out.

Nights like that, I wondered why I decided to pay my own way through school.

The next day: pre-med biology at 8:30, anatomy/ physiology at 10, and my Czech language lab at 12:15. Not that I knew anything about Czech when I signed up for the class, but it sounded cool. The language lab usually went fifty minutes—which meant that, if I ran out the minute class ended, I had a twenty-five-minute break to eat lunch before I had to be on the highway, en route to my other job.

Hey, I told you I was paying my own way through school.

I didn't say that dollar twenty-five tips from family-fun restaurants were going to do it.

"Distant."

I batted my eyes. I rolled back my shoulders and gazed into the distance.

"Shy, seductive."

I flicked my fingernails in the air, outstretched, like someone was going to kiss my hand. My body leaned back and my breasts rose, firming the outline of my camisole under the drape top.

"Enthusiastically bored."

I shrugged my shoulders. I looked at the camera dead-on, the way modeling schools always tell you never to do. I flashed the exact look I was feeling right then.

I had only been doing this for a few months, but really, I'd been doing it for my whole life. I never used to believe those prodigy kids on TV who were brilliant at playing piano from the start, but now, I knew how it was to be naturally good at something. My first language was body language, and modeling was the first thing that's ever come natural to me. I felt slightly guilty, making money for doing practically nothing—and then I remembered how I felt whenever I went out with Velma and she picked up the check, having inherited zillions of dollars by doing *literally* nothing, and I started to feel less guilty.

The photographer flashed a couple more times. He told me I'm perfect, I'm beautiful, all the things I already knew.

I took it with dead eyes and a smile like honey.

"'Enthusiastically bored'? What does that mean, like bored squared?"

Velma listened to me complain about my day.

Velma was the only person I ever let myself complain to, but then, she was also the only person I walked around in my underwear in front of. I mean, aside from the photo shoots—and none of that stuff was under-wear I actually *wore*, anyway. Tonight we were at

Velma's apartment, in the living room, lying head next to head on a shared pillow where our bodies met in the middle of the couch.

"It's what photographers *say*," I told Velma. "They don't *mean* anything. They just need to feel like artists. What you do is, you ignore everything they tell you and you look however the hell you want to look."

"Maybe I could be a model." Velma's eyes twinkled. She looked away for a second.

"Velm, why would you want to be a model? You've got everything right now. Modeling only messes with your head."

Velma was shorter than me, but smarter. My new agent would call her a sidekick type, but that's because he'd never stick around long enough to listen to Velma speak. She was clever, and smart, and sleazily, wonderfully inappropriate. She was also in her first year of college, for business.

She was also richer than me.

My father worked for her grandparents. He was a doctor. They'd first hired him years ago, and since then, they'd become his biggest fans and most frequent clients. They would call him for the craziest things, like a twisted fingernail or pets with colds. They always called my father about their pets. It was the weirdest thing. It was like, even with their zillions of dollars, they'd never heard of veterinary medicine. But they figured, if my dad was so good with humans, he would know how to make anything better. He never complained, just told them what he knew, to the best of his knowledge. He never billed them for those things, the weird aliments and off-kilter pet questions, but they always sent him a check anyway.

And that's how I grew up. Living in the shadow of someone a full head shorter, but never quite minding it. Velma was a notorious attention-grabber, and so I got to live a lot more inside my head, reciting times tables to myself while she kept up all the boring conversations with all the boring boys that we were supposed to find *deathly* interesting.

I could handle the modeling stuff—those egotistical photographers I was just beginning to get used to, the ad executives on head-trips who always wanted to take you to snappy dinners and dance with you, just so they know their product is well represented. They wanted to smell their signature perfume drifting off your well-tanned hundred and twenty dollars-an-hour neck and watch you pull away and parlay their kisses into the air. I had to keep reminding myself, the hundred and twenty dollar hours only came one hour every few weeks, and they would soon melt into days upon days of waitress-wage hours at the restaurant.

If she modeled, Velma would take them so seriously. She'd ask for their phone numbers and let them go all the way with her. That was the kind of girl she was.

I knew they were kidding, but there were more important things to know. I knew how to pull away, but I also knew how to make them feel okay about it.

Velma's phone rang. She checked the display, waited a second, and then hit the Ignore button.

"What's that about?" I asked. Velma and I hung out enough that we didn't need to worry about taking phone calls while the other was around.

"It's Nikos. I met him at the AIDS benefit concert last week after Tyler took me to dinner. He keeps calling me. Nikos doesn't know about Christopher yet, and I want to break it to him gently."

"God, you are such a player!"

Velma made this horrified shriek. "I am *not*!"

"Then how do you work yourself into all this stuff?"

"I don't know! It just happens." She jabbed at the buttons of her cell phone, scrolling through her contacts list, or maybe through her date book. "Oh, I don't know how to handle it. I never know how to handle boys. Maybe you're right about modeling; I'll never be swift like you are."

"*Now* you're being lame. You get yourself out of more complicated situations than anyone else I know gets *into* In the first place. It's time to face facts, Velm. You're a player."

Velma's face contracted even harder. She couldn't believe I said it, even though she knew it was so true.

"And besides," I added softly. "I hate going out with guys I meet at shoots. They stare at me weird and never look in my eyes when I'm talking and they never even *listen* to what I'm saying."

It's not that Velma didn't get play when she was in high school—she got plenty, but she never got *public* play. Guys got with her like *crazy* in private, but nobody wanted to walk around school holding her hand. Now, things had changed, except, in Velma's mind, she was still that timid girl who couldn't find a date to the prom. I kept telling Velma she was a stud, and she didn't believe me, but one day, I knew, she was gonna realize just how much power she had over boys.

And, that day, Velma was going to become absolutely dangerous.

Velma's phone rang off the hook that night. First, it was the new guys she met last weekend, then an even newer guy she met Monday night, and then Christopher, Velma's I-can't-believe-it's-not boyfriend, calling to find out how her weekend was and cross-examine her about why they didn't hang out more. In books, girls always come off sounding like the pathetic ones, but in my experience, it was always boys who got all neurotic and clingy.

I could hear Christopher's voice dripping with electronic sap from across the room.

I knew it was going to be a long conversation, so I planted myself at Velma's desk, went online, and started doing my work for class. Microbiology was a review of most stuff I'd known before—nervous systems, blood vessels, antibodies, disease—I mean, systems I'd had memorized for *years*. My father used to read me to sleep on this stuff. But I was so not falling into the trap of being a college freshman. I was sure my prof had his own way of teaching micro, and he probably didn't know as much as I did, but I knew when to take orders and let the teacher call the shots.

Velma's phone voice got louder.

"I am NOT yelling at you!!!" she screamed.

Then she got even louder.

Velma's yelling was impossible to ignore, and I was pretty sure Christopher was yelling on the other line too, and finally Velma said, "That's it, Christopher. I'm breaking up with you!" and there was dead silence.

At first I thought she'd hung up.

After a minute, I realized, she was listening to him talk. She nodded, *hmm*ed, and batted her eyelashes through the rest of the conversation. Finally, Velma said, "Okay, fine, I'll think it over. But it's going to be the same. Yes, you can call in ten minutes . . . . Yes, I *promise* I'll pick up."

She tossed the phone onto the couch.

"Oh my *Lord*," Velma said. "He wants me to think it over before I break up. He says I need time to breathe. Can you believe it? Time to breathe. I mean, he *knows* how big my lungs are. He said, he wants me to break up with him with a clear head."

"And you let him get away with that?" I said.

She shot me a look.

"You *are* letting him get away with that."

"If it makes him feel better," Velma's eyes shone. "Besides, it's the last thing I'll ever have to do for him."

Poor Velma. She tried and she tried and all she ever did was end up with losers.

"Do you want to talk?" I offered.

Velma considered this. "Yeah," she said. "Yeah, I think I do."

She walked over to the computer where I was working, closed the window with my homework, and opened her instant-message program.

"What are you doing?" I said.

"Looking for Matty," said Velma.

I shrugged, about to cut loose with a great snide, ball-busting remark. Instead, my eyes glazed over, and I went out on the porch.

Matty was Velma's internet best friend. They'd been talking to each other for almost two years, but they'd never actually met. At first I thought it was the weirdest thing in the world, but, geez, weirder things happen all the time. Matty lived up north, in New York City. He worked for a magazine, and he did stuff with computers. Like Velma, he had a busy social life, but also like Velma, sometimes he retreated from his scene and stayed home at night and wrote and surfed online and philosophized about life with her. Velma could have flown up there any time to visit—it would take literally three hours just to meet him, say hi, have a round of drinks, and fly back—but she always told me, she wanted to keep him at arm's length. That's where she decided he was most comfortable.

I could understand that. Arm's length is where I've kept every guy I've ever dated. Pretty much everyone I've ever known, too. Even Velma, sometimes, when she got too intense.

Atlanta by night looks like a river of lights, dull yellow and close to the ground. I've been all over the city—my father used to drive me around for hours, zigzagging down street after street, telling me so many stories that they couldn't all be true. Other cities, I've been in them two days, and it's felt like I owned them. But I've never felt like I owned Atlanta. Watching the people on the streets at every hour of the night, walking across neighborhoods for a social call at three A.M., or to switch clubs—this isn't a city you can control. You might get fluent in Atlanta, but you'll never be able to own it.

I stared out in the distance for a bit, trying to see as far as I could. Then I sighed, turned my back on the city, and went inside to rejoin the world.

Velma was still online with Matty. She was typing animatedly, watching the screen the whole time for a reaction.

I passed the desk, walked to the couch, and sunk in.

I could read little snips of Velma's conversation from where I sat. It looked exactly like I expected it to: Velma complaining. Velma's words showed up in red. There were lines and lines of Velma, punctuated sporadically by a point or a comment from Matty in blue. He sounded like such the peanut gallery. "He needs you more than you need him." "You go, girl." "Don't worry what guys think, *we* both know you're fab." I mean, really. Who even *says* "fab" anymore?

"How's your online boyfriend, Velm?" I said, picking up my Coke. I sipped through the straw until the bottle bubbled emptiness back at me.

"Matty is great, thank you very much. And he is *so* not my online boyfriend."

"Why not? You've got enough real ones."

"For your information," said Velma curtly, entering another line of text, "Matty and I are just friends. Lord knows I could use one of them about now."

"A friend? Just tell me when I should start acting hurt."

"A *just*-friend. As in, a guy who is not after me."

"Oh well. You're not gonna find that around here." I vainly slurped at the bottom of my Coke. "I just want you for your body."

I burst out laughing at my own joke. If I had one Achilles' heel, that would be it. I might be the cleverest person on the planet, but I have the weakest sense of humor. I crack up at the stupidest things. I even crack up when I *tell* jokes.

Velma's phone buzzed. She picked it up and checked the display. "Oh, now, wouldn't you have guessed *that* in your sleep," she said, flipping it open. "It's Christopher."

"And you're actually going to *talk* to him?" I demanded.

Velma made hushing sounds at me while she answered. In the sweetest voice imaginable, she said, "Christopher, darling, I'm just so terribly sorry, but my rational mind agrees with the rest of me. Get bent."

You could hear him arguing on the other line. And—after holding out for a few minutes—you could see Velma's expressive face listening to his arguments, folding into a sympathetic frown.

She looked at me while she fiddled with the sapphire ring on her pinky finger—which, I remembered, Christopher had given her for her last birthday.

It was going to be a long conversation.

"What am I supposed to do, then?" I hissed.

"Talk to Matty," said Velma.

I sat down at the computer desk. I had every intention of closing right out of Matty and getting back to the exhilaration of microbiology lab. But something stopped me.

Okay, so it wasn't *something* that stopped me.

It was Matty.

This desolate, lonely-looking cursor was blinking on and off, right after he'd typed to Velma: "you don't have to take his call. you don't owe anything to him but you owe a shitload to yourself." That was pretty good advice, I had to admit. It was exactly what I would have said, if I was that quick.

"Too late," I typed back. "Velma has officially thrown herself overboard."

Without missing a beat—a *beat*—the guy types to me, "it's okay. i figured as much. all i can really do is her life preserver, and sooner or later, she'll swim back to shore."

"'Her life preserver'? What are you, an Impressionist poet or something?"

"no—i just tell her good things & make her feel better about herself. i'm like velma's best gay friend. only i'm not gay."

"And you're REALLY not interested in her?"

"swear to god. who is this, anyway?"

"She didn't tell you?"

"she *never* tells me these things."

"Well, welcome to Velma Land."

"thanks, it's good to be here. population: me and—?"

"Candy."

"whoa—you're *candy*."

"What's that supposed to mean??"

"nothing. just, velma's said sooo many things about you."

"Jesus, I have a reputation on the internet?"

"only good things, candy, i promise."

I smiled.

In spite of myself, I was smiling at him.

We talked. We talked, pretending we were talking about Velma, but that pretension dropped away like an old exoskeleton. We talked and it was playful, clever, slightly dirty but in that wonderful torturous way where you're one-upping each other, like daring each other to kiss—*"you first." "No, you first."*—until one of us actually does. No, it wasn't that sexual, but it *was*. Not, like, overtly or anything, but it was so there, floating just below the letters on the screen, like we were about to jump straight in through the computer screens and *ravage* each other. I swear it. I mean, I've hooked up with people where it hasn't been as intense as us typing.

As intense as typing to a guy named Matty whom I had never seen.

"yeah?" he wrote. "how would you like to?"

"To see you?" I typed back.

"(shrug.)"

"What do you want me to do, click on my video camera or something?"

"no!! i mean, like, you *can*, but—come here."

I bit my lip.

"To New York?" I typed.

"mm-hmm."

I could actually do that.

I was awash in my own thoughts. Velma—in the corner, her voice growing louder by the minute—wouldn't think twice about skipping across the country, or multiple countries, even, in order to meet a boy she found fascinating.

And I was definitely feeling fascinated by this conversation.

"I could do that," I wrote. In my head, the situation was already taking shape. A nice, quiet, anonymous few days in New York—no pressure, no social obligations, just hanging out with Matty. He seemed low-maintenance enough, and if for some reason he tried something and I didn't want him to, I could just come back home. All I'd have to do, I calculated at that moment, was ask Velma for a loan. Mildly embarrassing, especially considering the circumstances, but I could do it.

I'd hesitated. Matty could smell it. "but what about your job?" he asked.

"I could skip it."

"and school?"

Damn. He'd called my bluff. My fingers froze in mid-typing position. I mean, I could always get fired and get another job, and my friends wouldn't miss me for one round of partying. But school. I was obsessed with being a good student, with proving everybody wrong who thought I was just another blond coasting by on my looks, and my inner geek had just gotten called out. I couldn't do it.

I could tell, Matty could tell. Whatever was unnatural about this—whatever was making this more than words on a screen—it was working in both directions.

And that was kind of a cool feeling to have.

" . . . ."

"wow," he wrote. "velma said you were never at a loss for words."

"I'm *not*. I mean—well, usually. I guess there's a first time for everything."

"then you'll come?"

"But I'm *good* about school. I have *never* missed school before."

"well, there's a first time for everything . . . ."

Velma, on the phone, was beginning to speak with an air of finality.

"Look, I should go and take care of Our Girl," I told him. "And—yeah—I guess I am serious about school. But give me a chance. Maybe I'll just show up after classes. ;) "

"really???"

"Maybe."

"but really maybe?"

"Really maybe."

"so . . . bye?" he said.

"Bye for now," I told him.

"bye for now," agreed Matty.

I closed off. I went to Velma, who was getting off the phone. My first instinct was to fire a barrage of questions about Matty. Was he in school? Was his voice as playful as it sounded from his writing? Did he have a girlfriend? But I stopped thinking those things the second Velma hung up from Christopher. Her eyes were bleary and red, streaked with tears.

"He still wants to make out," she said. "But he doesn't want to *go* out with me."

"But, Velms," I said. "Isn't that exactly what you wanted?"

Velma nodded. Her head fell on my shoulder, and she started to sob.

I shook my head. I never did pretend to understand Velma and her mood swings. Sometimes, all I can do is let her know I'm there.

I hugged her and walked her into her room and tucked her into her big down bed. Then I climbed in and fell asleep with her, holding her hand like a mother would.

The Just-Friend

(3)

I woke up earlier than Velma, jumpy and restless. The sun was just rising, poking thin lasers of light through the clouds and along the hardwood floors. I jumped out of bed to take a bath, stopped halfway through her living room, and checked the computer.

Matty was online.

"I was hoping you'd be here," I typed.

"geez, can't you get enough of me?" he wrote back. "don't you have stuff to do today?"

I did. I had my microbiology lab today that I still had to prepare for, an essay due in English that I was probably going to write during the slow parts of the micro lab, and a photo session for a swimsuit catalog that started at six and would probably last through the night.

I had plenty of stuff to do that day. I probably didn't even have time for a bath.

But I talked to Matty for half an hour anyway.

I could hear the cheeky grin in his voice. Making fun of me, but in a good way. Nobody ever made fun of me. Everyone was either intimidated by me or they wanted things from me. I tried to think, apart from Velma, about the last time I had an innocent good time just hanging out. I couldn't come up with anything.

Then again, I was working on three hours' sleep, maybe less. I don't know why I woke up so early. I never really sleep. I don't trust myself when I'm not busy.

It took me twelve minutes to get to class from home. I gave myself twenty, just because I liked being in the front row. I couldn't help it, I was a total nerd exhibitionist—I loved looking smart. The guys in math classes will prejudge you in a second for having long hair and a miniskirt, and I always liked answering the questions faster than they did.

Today, I left at exactly 9:18 A.M. After talking to Matty for longer than either of us planned on. I even told him about my plans—"do they check you out during class and lose their place in the book?" he asked. "Mm-hmm," I typed back. "that is so sexy," he said—we were both laughing, I could tell.

Until 9:18 A.M, that is.

At school, I couldn't find a parking spot. The lot was full, and all my safe spaces were taken. Finally I parked next to a fire hydrant, trusting that there wouldn't be any fires happening for the next hour and a half. Why else would they make those extra-long hoses, anyway?

So I got to class, slid in just as my name was being called on roll. I raised my hand extra high. I smiled at the T.A. He smiled back, flirty and eager, and I averted my eyes—*as if*—and pulled out my textbook.

Today we were learning pressure points. You know all those jokes about surgeons and steady hands? When you operate near a pressure point, that's when you're not joking about steady hands anymore. The jugular vein is a tiny vein on the human neck that wriggles like a worm in the sun. If you pierce it, the patient has anywhere between ten seconds and ten minutes to live. Depending on direction and depth of the cut, that's a huge margin—but, once cut, it is a certainty: he will die.

I wore my old-school Gucci glasses during class. Thick, powdery frames. They silhouetted my eyes in thin cupolas of glass in the arcing shape of narrowed eyebrows. When I was eleven, glasses transformed me into a complete dork. Nobody wanted me at their lab table.

Not today. My skirt was shorter than the hem of my lab coat. I could feel the warm, crablike feel of guys' eyes on my legs.

I turned around slowly. I was controlling every tenor of the movement of my head. Wiley Finn's eyes, small and pupily, flickered but they didn't come off my legs. His dark eyebrows rose like an invitation. Wiley was a total stud. He knew he could have any girl. He didn't have to apologize for looking. I scowled, which I think turned him on.

I twisted back around and focused on the book.

Girls—popular girls especially—were never supposed to be good at math. I loved math. I could always feel the numbers flow through my head like water.

It was the same with biology, now. All I had to do was read this textbook and I understood it. Like, I *knew*. I got lost in the professor's lecture and forgot all about Wiley Finn until the end of class, when he bumped into me on purpose.

"Hey, Candy," he said. "Feel like grabbing some beers with me tonight?"

"Actually, no," I said. "Thanks for asking, I'll see you Thursday."

He sidestepped me. "Why?" he asked. "Going to a model shoot?"

Wiley said that at the same time I was saying, "I'm going to a model shoot."

He pulled back, stunned, like he hadn't actually thought it would be the truth. "Are you really, like, a model?"

"Yeah, and you know what else? I have to go."

"That's so cool. You should model for me some time."

"Pick up the new *Glamour*," I shot back. I turned and left for class, leaving Wiley Finn scratching his head with those rich-boy manicured fingernails of his.

The director of the photo shoot clapped his hands together briskly. You could tell he was not in a mood to be patient.

Neither was I, actually. My car was being towed when I finally got back to it, and I had to convince the owner of the towing service, who was a friend of my father's, to call the trucking guy and make him not tow my car away. I got to the session a minute before make-up call started, and I *hated* cutting it close.

"Listen up, girls. Today we're going to do this fast and efficient. No wasted poses. It's a big day for the Kiss the Reign Cosmetics campaign. Preston Reign is coming to personally check in on the ad shoots."

The girl next to me bubbled over, clapping her hands like she'd suddenly been nominated for an Oscar. I yawned and studied the area for something to do, because I knew she was about to start fawning and I wanted a distraction. I dug in my bag and found a Rubik's Cube just as she opened her mouth.

"Oh. My. *God*. I can't believe Preston is coming *here*! Like, today! You *do* know he's the heir to one of the largest fortunes in North America, don't you?"

I shot a dead evil glare at her. Yes, I did know that. I felt like pointing out how *my* best friend was the heir to another of the largest fortunes in the country, too, but that would just be lame.

"Yes, well, he's *also* a notorious playboy," said Phasia, another model, who was already dressed in her lingerie for the first shoot. She had long manicured nails that looked like claws, and her eyes looked predatory ,too. "Last year, his favorite football team was losing, so he bought their main rival and fired the coach and quarterback. And *Newsweek* just said that he's not right in the you-know-what." She tapped her head to indicate it.

"Yeah, well, I'm sure he'd do just fine. For *me,* that is," said the first model perkily.

Phasia snorted.

So utterly un-model-like, I thought.

"There's a big *if* you're missing," she said dryly.

Most of the other girls there had expressions just like Phasia's—disinterested, but hungry just beneath the surface. Like, if Preston Reign asked another girl for her phone number, they'd be the first to offer their pen, and when she licked the tip, it would be laced with cyanide.

Yes, this was what working with models was like. I thought about Steaks & Co., and daydreams of two-dollar tips danced in my head.

"Candy Cohen! You're on!" the DP called.

I dropped the cube, shed my robe, strode over to the set, and got ready to play backup to a bottle of perfume.

"You know, you're very good at what you do."

I glanced up from my textbook, my entertainment between takes, and into my makeup mirror. A guy about my age was standing behind me, wearing a tuxedo, his hair curly and glossed up.

"At standing still? Thanks. I trained for three months in Rome, watching the statues."

"Rome, huh? I have a house there."

"I'm sure you do." I kept my gaze averted, watching Phasia and two other models writhing on silk sheets as the photographer snapped away.

"You're so fascinating. I've never met someone who talked back to their employer before." He rested his chin in his fist, gazing at me unabashedly.

I turned my head a little. "I'm your employee?"

"I'm sorry, I'm being rude. I haven't even introduced myself. My name is Preston." He extended his hand.

I ignored it. "Actually, Preston, I'm a freelancer. Which means I have an agency, and you hire my agency. Which means *I* work for them, and *they* work for you."

"So what does that make us?"

"Absolutely nothing."

"That's good to know," he declared

"Why is that?"

"Because my lawyers tell me I should never ask an employee on a date."

"Then maybe you shouldn't ask," I said softly.

I let the barest trace of a smile peek through. Then I turned completely, away from my makeup mirror, to face him dead-on.

"I'm sorry, Preston," I said. "I doubt you're accustomed to being turned down, but I keep a very busy calendar these days."

"I can tell you don't work for me. I'm accustomed to being the cleverest person in my office."

I smiled again, full-on this time. For that, I took his hand—which was still out and extended—and I shook it. "Still no," I told him. "But I appreciate the compliment."

"Well, you're right about one thing," he said. "I'm not accustomed to being turned down." With that, he stood, straightened his bowtie, and took three steps toward the door, still facing me. "It was a pleasure meeting you, Candy. I'll talk to you shortly, I trust."

"How do you know I'll keep talking to you at all?" I said under my breath. He should have been too far away to hear it but he was paying attention.

Preston smiled condescendingly, like he was explaining advanced math to a child. "Because nobody tells me no."

"Oh, a challenge. Watch me."

I swiveled around in my stool and looked away.

These were not things I should care about. Usually I could dismiss a boy and he'd be done with me, off flirting with the next model. Especially if the room was full of them. When I told a guy *no* twice in one conversation, he almost never walked away without his face turned beet-red with embarrassment, feeling like I was laughing at him even though my face wouldn't show any of it. That was just how clever I was. Or, at least, that was how clever I made myself seem.

I turned in my chair, expecting Preston to evaporate into thin air, or float away on the coattails of some catty remark that he'd fling into the air, meant for me.

But he was still standing there. Staring into my makeup mirror, the length of his body in the background, just over my shoulder. His hands rested in his pockets, looking as cocksure and pleased with himself as could be. His reflection made eye contact with my reflection. His eyes looked at me with an intensity that felt supernatural, taking in the minutiae of my posture, memorizing every parabolic curve of my tussled hair.

I stiffened.

"So," he said, almost out the door. "How about dinner tomorrow night?"

"Sorry. I work tomorrow."

"That's not a problem," he said. "We can have dinner anyway."

I bit my lip—I was *so* about to say something very un-employee-like—but I glanced back into the mirror, and he was already gone.

I brushed a strand of hair out of my eyes. My finger touched my cheek. The slightest amount of foundation came off, and I rubbed it between my thumb and forefinger, mixing the powder together with the oil of my skin.

Suddenly, I felt very strange.

That night when I came home, Velma was already over at my apartment. She was watching a movie on the bigscreen TV with a couple of her friends from school. It had just hit the scary part, and when I opened the door, everybody screamed, Velma jumped off the couch, and a fountain of bright yellow popcorn streamed across my apartment, cascading down along the hardwood floor. Kernels rolled into the legs of my dinner table and bounced to a halt.

When everyone saw that it was me, we all had a big laugh and Velma turned off the TV. I sank into an easy chair, kicked off my heels, and sighed. All the pent-up exhaustion in my body leaked out.

Except of course I had to tell Velma what happened first, and the other girls listened in, too. Velma shrieked when she heard. "Oh my *God*!" she screamed. "I *cannot* be*lieve* you met Preston *Reign*! Was he as cute as he looks in *People*?"

"He's not bad," I shrugged. For Velma, meeting stars she already knew was no big deal. But the other ones, the unconnected stars who dip below the radar, was huge. I managed to wind her down and convince her that Preston was no big deal, and *cer*tainly not as cool as Matty. I figured it was safe to name-drop Matty, cause if Velma wanted me to explain my weird friendship with him, she'd have to explain her own weird friendship with him first.

The other girls squealed. They wanted to know who Matty was.

I scooped up my heels and walked to my bedroom, closing the door, leaving Velma to fend off their questions. Inside, I peeled off all of my clothes, dove under the goose down covers, and went straight to sleep.

But not without emailing Matty first.

A Nice Lunch and a Cheap Dinner

(4)

The next morning, I walked down the main campus throughway wearing my Tom Ford sunglasses, a new pink minidress, sparkly heels, and a B Fendi Buckle bag that was the exact same shade as my lipstick. You know those days when life just seems like the factory in *Willy Wonka*, your makeup goes on streakless, and you're walking on chocolate-flavored water? That's how today felt.

I'd just had a huge revelation about myself. Usually, after I have a crazy day, I always need to call Velma and tell her everything. But last night, life had seemed so empty and unsatisfying, even though Velma was right in the room.

And then, by the end of the night, it hadn't.

After I'd met Matty.

Well, not *met* Matty, but you know what I mean. And actually, it kind of did feel as though we were friends now. Not like we actually knew each other, either. But it felt like we'd shared an experience. Like we'd shared *something*.

In the morning—by the time I woke up—there was a new email sitting in my box.

I don't know what to say. It wasn't spectacular. It wasn't suave and self-assured like Preston, or sisterly and agreeable like Velma, and it wasn't what I expected Matty to write back, either. It was just a regular letter, funny and cute and flirty as hell, telling me about the last date *he* went on—the girl expected him to pay for everything, kept pushing away the check even when he told her he was horrible at math—"*How* much was it again?"—and he put down exactly half the money for their pizza.

"it was so much better than actually *paying* for the pizza," Matty wrote, "messing with her head to see whether i would pay for it or not. i mean, social norms are so messed up—just because that guy preston can usually get any girl's number, and now you didn't give it to him, he must think you're the hottest thing in the world. i mean, you *are*, of course. but not for any reason he could guess."

At first I wanted to be like, *where do you get off presuming that?*

But then I realized, he could tell it from my words. Just from our conversation. He was a writer. Words were everything to him.

For all I knew, Matty still didn't know what I looked like.

Between classes, I met my father for lunch at the University Club. Once a week he had some business to take care of in the city, and he'd drive in early and meet me for lunch. I ran across campus from my Czech lab. He was waiting there, sipping a glass of chardonnay that perfectly matched his camel-colored sport jacket. I slid into the chair and he could tell right away that I was giddy.

Yes—that was my father.

My father was the kind of man who didn't speak much, but it was almost impossible to put things past him. He was tall and thin, and he'd been balding forever, but it never seemed to hit a critical level. It looked natural on him. His face, thin and gaunt, a perpetual autumn complexion, pulled it off well. Most of my friends were ashamed to be seen with their parents, but I was proud of my father. He was a handsome dad.

He leaned forward and watched me read the menu. "What's the big news, then?" he asked.

"What big news do you mean?"

"Come on. You're more ebullient than I've seen you in months. It must be a boy."

I paused, my eyes flickering over the salad list. "Oh, Dad," I sighed.

"Stop pulling my leg, Candy. Make my lunch break worthwhile."

The waiter appeared. I gave my order and then I told my father about Preston Reign.

He nodded, but like he could see through me, like he expected something more. My father had heard of Preston—I mean, *everyone* had, his monthly clothes budget was as big as the national debt—but he didn't bat an eye. He waited until I was quite done explaining, dabbed his lips with his napkin, and said, "So that's the *first* guy."

"Yes. He seems very nice."

"Nice doesn't make the world go round, Candy."

I blushed the color of my dress. Then, in fits and giggles, I told him about Matty.

Well, I didn't tell him *about* Matty. Just little things— that he was Velma's friend, and from New York, and that he was a writer. And that I didn't quite know what or why, but when we talked, I got warm chills all over my skin.

As I talked, my father poured me a glass of wine. When I'd finished, he lifted up his glass and clinked it lightly against mine.

"What are you toasting to?" I asked, surprised. "To Matty?"

"Of course not," said my father. "Well, maybe to him, too. But to you. To all the decisions you'll make. And all the incisions you're already making."

I thought that was a Freudian slip, but like I said, my father was clever. That afternoon in my lab, we spent three hours learning how to make incisions in patients, and it all kept coming back to the jugular. You don't want to hit the jugular by accident. Just the idea that veins hold my entire blood supply scared me out of my brains. They're so narrow and small, especially on someone as skinny as me. I thought of the last time a boy kissed my neck and it made me shiver, how close he was to my jugular.

Before class ended, some guy tried to ask me out. I thought it was Wiley again, and I kept saying "No, Wiley," but then it turns out his name was Marco and he'd never met me before. I apologized politely, but then I decided that maybe I was stressing out too much and I should go to the school computer lab before work and see about chatting up Matty.

"hi honey. what did you learn in school today?" he typed.

"Veins."

"tell me a story about veins, then."

"Ugh. I don't want to. I'll tell you about anything else in the world. I *never* want to think about veins again."

"then tell me about your heart."

"Don't you get all cheesy ass on me."

"i'm not. i never say *heart* when i mean cheesy stuff. i love the idea of actual hearts, though: the squirmy things with all the veins sticking out. that those are what keep us alive. if i gave you my heart, that's what it would look like. not some dumb velvet pillow with lumps and a point at the bottom."

"Veins don't stick out of your heart. Those are vessels."

"can i tell you how much i love the word *vessel*? it's like it's taking your blood to a faraway land. to europe."

"Europe isn't that great. I'd rather go to the moon."

"i'd just like to sail. no matter where i end up. as long as i do it in a vessel."

I could talk all day to that kid. If only I didn't have responsibilities. I daydreamed about vessels, but I paid attention to my responsibilities.

I said good-bye, and it felt too quick. That was the moment I knew I was digging him seriously—because I've never had to say good-bye to anyone before. Usually, I just walk out the door without a second glance.

Velma always teased me about working at a restaurant. Even if I was paying for my own college, she argued, why would I ever want to get grease in my hair and hamburger under my nails? I had my modeling.

The truth was, it wasn't about money. I needed to have something that kept me humble. I wanted to be able to walk out of a shoot, never turn back, and know that I would still have something to keep me busy—and the busier I was, the better I felt about myself.

Work that night was absolutely crazy.

I was in high spirits. I was jotting down orders like gunfire, throwing down every meal as it came. One of the waiters had called in sick and I had double duty, twelve tables, which was usually a nightmare.

Not tonight, though. Tonight, I was on top of every one of them. I did not mix up mustard and mayonnaise on the finicky businessmen's pre-spread burgers. I got every salad to the table at the same time. I was so damn good, maybe for the first time ever.

Then I saw the hostess having a conversation with a tall, well-dressed man with long, curly hair.

Preston.

She seated him by the window at a table for two. She laid down a menu, and then she walked away.

I went up to her. "Lainie, what are you *doing*?"

She smiled enthusiastically and did a little cha-cha dance with her hips. "He said he was having dinner with you."

"But I'm working!"

"He said this would explain everything." Lainie held up a hundred-dollar bill.

I grabbed for it, purely to spite her.

She pulled it away and tucked it in the pocket of her shirt. "It really *did* explain everything," she said. "Have a good dinner."

Preston sat in an empty corner of the restaurant, away from all the depressing-looking businessmen and the families with their French-fry fights. He was surveying the menu and sipping a glass of Perrier. I had no doubt he was wondering to himself what I was doing working here, at a place where the blue-plate special was called the *Double Trouble Burger Deluxx* and waffle-cut fries were seventy-five cents extra.

I pulled the chair out, smoothed my skirt, and sat down opposite Preston. I angled my chair so I could jump out the second the manager saw me in customer mode. Not that Preston wouldn't weasel me out of it. And not that I was actually planning to dine with him.

"What are you doing here?"

He didn't even pause.

"Pursuing the woman of my dreams." He flashed an ironic smile, and I couldn't tell whose leg he was trying to pull more—mine or his own.

"I'll tell you right now, clichés turn me off at least as bad as a guy showing up to flirt with me at work."

"Well look at that, I'm batting two for two. Tell me you don't also work in the strip club I'm going to hit after dinner?"

I shook my head. "You're on your own for that."

"Too bad, I bet you'd make it a cool ride."

"Preston," I said, trying to keep my voice kind, "has any girl ever told you that your conversation skills are more like conversation *kills*?"

When I told him that, he just shook his head sadly and chuckled. Chuckled, and not in a nice way. I don't think anyone who *chuckles* does it nicely. He smoothed his hair—not that it wasn't already smooth as silk—and touched my hand with his.

"I blame society. Not for my desire—that is, of course my own—but for the cruel and inevitable ways that, unfortunately, I manifest this desire. Beautiful, intelligent girls are taught to make themselves unreachable, as though saying *no* to me is their own stylized way of saying *try harder*. Clever entrepreneurial young men—and I hope you don't deem it pretentious for me to count myself among this group—are taught that, with proper determination and drive, we can achieve anything we wish, whether in business, socially, or—in our quest for the perfect relationship—of turning that *no* into a *yes*."

"Dude," I said, "you sound like a conquistador."

"Well, I do have three yachts," Preston smiled. "Just like Columbus."

I stood up.

"Sit down, please. What can I order you?" asked Preston, perusing the menu idly. "Don't worry about money. The twelve-dollar steak will hardly break my bank."

"I'm a vegetarian," I said icily as I towered over him. "Besides, I'm *working*, in case you hadn't noticed."

"I think I prefer it when you stand around like a Roman statue for work. Or when you work for me." He took a delicate sip of his Perrier.

"Check, please," I called, loud enough so that if I was the waitress on duty, I would have pissed myself off.

*

*   *

After that fiasco, I still had to work another three hours. I watched Preston Reign exit slowly, slip into his limo that had been waiting at the front of the restaurant for half an hour, and cruise out the driveway and onto the freeway before I started clearing the dishes and wiping up the table where he sat. The few customers we had were all staring at me.

I got home, smelly and disgusting, my hair in more knots than a Greek myth. I felt awful. All I wanted was to jump in the shower and feel my pores unclog and melt down the drain.

But as soon as I got home, I got that rush of excitement.

I knew someone who wouldn't tell me that I smelled.

Matty: "how was work?"

"Creepy. How was homework?"

"couldn't get it done fast enough. you still up for Saturday?"

"You think I'd miss it for anything?"

" 'anything'? ;)"

"Okay, punko. Just stay right there."

It was Friday morning. My plane left tomorrow afternoon, and to be honest, I was glad. Atlanta was giving me the creeps.

Friday afternoon. I wondered what he looked like. Velma had never talked about what he looked like. Should I ask him to send me his picture? Should I expect him to volunteer it? It didn't matter, I'd see him soon enough. I felt this expectancy pounding. It wasn't like expecting to be voted prom queen or expecting your father to invite your favorite pitcher from the Atlanta Braves to your birthday party. This was something older than that, something deeper. Remember those old movies from the '80s where the main girl just *knows* that the geeky kid and the slick, well-dressed superhero are the same person? It was that kind of expectation.

I was ready for destiny. Or something like destiny. I was ready for something bigger than modeling and waitressing and college.

Friday night I arrived home from work, exhausted and perspiring, and fell straight to bed fully dressed.

I'm probably the lightest sleeper ever. My father used to tell me he'd come in to find me in all sorts of weird positions, sitting straight up in bed, or my legs stretched up against the wall. Sometimes I even slept with my eyes open.

That night, I woke with a start.

I thought I'd heard something.

I'm always hearing things. A moth batting wings against the window could wake me. In the summer, I hear the chirp of crickets and *that* wakes me, too.

On instinct, my hand jabbed out in the dark. I yanked the tin chain. The old lamp flickered on.

A man sat on the edge of my bed.

"What the hell are you doing here?"

The words couldn't come out of my mouth fast enough.

"I missed you, Candy. I couldn't sleep because I was thinking about you. I thought I'd come over and tell you."

I snatched the blankets up over my body. "Okay, you've told me. Now leave."

*"Can*dy . . .*"

"Go away."

He leaned closer. "I thought you'd be flattered."

"I'm finished being flattered."

"Talk to me!"

His fists grasped the bed frame. They rattled it, hard.

My bedside table shook. So did the floor, and the framed pictures of Klimt, Escher, and early-era Madonna hanging on the wall. The lamp flickered on and off.

I climbed backwards out of bed, away from where Preston was leering over me, and I stood. I was still in my clothes from work. Thank God for small mercies.

"Look," I said, "if you want to make another appointment with me, you can do it through my agency. Although, if this is any indication, I probably won't feel like working with you very much in the future."

I walked over toward the door.

"You don't want to walk out that door," Preston said. His voice had calmed a little. He was sitting on my bed.

"I think I do."

He sat on my bed—on the edge of my comforter, the corner where the blankets were still tucked in—and smoothed down the area next to him. "Come here, Candy. Sit on your bed with me. Let's talk a little. I'm sure we can find a way to get along."

"You sleaze."

"Only if you want me to be." He leered at me.

"I can't believe this."

"I can be very gentlemanly, if you'd rather." He loosened his tie and unbuttoned his collar a notch.

"I'm getting out of here," I said, swinging my bedroom door open.

Three burly, gorilla-ish men stood in my living room. They were wearing tuxedos and sunglasses.

Their hands were clasped around pistols.

Real pistols. Pistols that did not look like water guns.

"I *told* you not to go out there!" Preston screamed. He sounded like a totally different person. His face was bright red, and suddenly, instead of his Prince Charming overtures, he was broadcasting the Evil Stepmother loud and clear.

"Who *are* you, Dr. Evil?" I yelled back. I breathed hard, trying to steady myself and not freak out, because if I freaked out, I'd lose it. And right now did not seem like a good time to lose it.

The guys in the living room just stood there. Their expressions didn't change at all.

Preston walked over, shut the door, and looked at me, a mixture of piteous and adoring. "I'm sorry, baby," he said. "I just wanted to impress you. Can we start over again?"

"This is not the way to start over," I said.

"Can I kiss you?"

"Are you totally insane?"

He leaned over. He was actually going to kiss me. His breath smelled like turpentine and expensive breath mints with the slightest hint of steak. And I know he was my age, but he had these veins in his forehead that bulged out, big like worms, and I wanted to run but there were men with guns in my living room.

My mother always used to ask after the boys I dated, did they come from a good enough family, were they richer than we were. She would have loved Preston.

Good thing she also got me kung fu lessons.

I jammed two fingers into a pressure point right below his ear.

The vein throbbed twice, quick. His mouth opened wide but no scream came out. Good. That meant I'd hit him in the right place. My fingers dug in farther and he toppled onto the soft carpet, nice and silent. I pressed so hard, he didn't even have time to scream.

I looked around. *Think fast, Candy, think fast—*

Out of the corner of my eye, I saw the door swing open.

Not fast enough.

The Men in Black sprung into action. There were three of them, all varying weights, sizes, and shapes.

The only thing they had in common was they were all bigger than I was.

The first one came running through the door, screaming like a broken car alarm. He was tall, stout, and slick. He had wraparound sunglasses and a six-inch switchblade in his hand.

You know how they say, once you learn to ride a bike, you never forget?

Well, I guess that's how kung fu works, too.

Before I knew what I was doing, my torso angled back and my left leg swung into a battle kick. It connected with his knuckles in the air. He yelped. The fingers of his right hand shot open, and the knife leaped from his grasp.

The knife sailed across the room, whistled, and landed with a dull *thud* into the middle of my Madonna poster—*Like A Virgin* tour, original, and did I mention it was signed?

"You bastard," I spat out.

The guy was still clutching his hand from the kick.

His eyes followed me, though, plotting. His body tightened, knees close, elbows pointed like a tiger. He flexed his upper body tight, ready for my next move.

I shot out my fist. My palm was level and my knuckles curled back.

When you hold your hand like that, it creates a flat board of force. If levered against a solid object, it sends the object reeling straight back in the air.

I slammed it right into his chest.

He crashed into the other two guys. They were waiting for their chance at me, unable to get through the door with their friend there.

Now that I'd cleared him, it was open season.

The first came at me with a handgun. He wasn't going to shoot it, I knew that. If he did, the police would be all over the apartment, like Velma at a Marc Jacobs sample sale. I was still worried, though. Shooting guns was one thing, but a gun is still hard and metal and it will knock you out cold.

He swung the gun through the air.

I ducked.

The weight of the pistol threw him into my bureau.

I spun around, slipping my body into an offensive pose. My arms moved in vertical circles, gathering up my chi. My hands pressed together, evenly, methodically. My lungs were shaking. I had to be calm.

The third guy had had time to prepare. His knife and gun were both out, and one was coming at me, too fast to pull away. Instead I leaned into him, taking him by surprise, throwing my weight into him and crashing him down to the floor. The knife nicked my arm.

I screamed.

No, I didn't. I felt my body about to scream. But it was just nervous energy. My need to let something out. In that single charged second of kinetic frenzy after the knife cut the flesh on my forearm, I let it all spill out into a punch.

I punched him.

No kung fu now. This was just me and my pissed-offness. My fist slammed into his face, throwing his oh-so-truckstop sunglasses across the room and his nose back and blood simply spurting all over the place, like a surfboard cutting the water. A graceful arc of red splattered across my room.

I glanced over at the window.

As the official Worst Night Ever, tonight still had some consolation prizes in store for me.

I grabbed a pair of discarded heels from the floor, climbed on to the fire escape, and jumped down to the street. Of course, I ran straight to Velma's apartment. It was the only place I could think of going.

She answered the door dressed in a bathrobe straight out of a PBS special, frilly grandmother lace up to her neck. "What happened?" she gasped, seeing the scrapes on my arms.

"A knife wound or two. Mostly I just crashed into a building," I managed to croak, my voice shaking. "Preston came by. He's even crazier than I thought."

"'Knife wounds'?" was all Velma could manage.

"Yeah. Big ones, too. They had guns, too, but I guess they were mostly for show. Tell me again why I never have boyfriends?"

"How—" she was still shaking. "How did you manage to fight them off?"

"Remember my kung fu classes?"

Velma's face suddenly snapped into a brand of recognizable confusion. "But I thought you never paid attention," she said.

"I lied. I was trying to sound cool."

Her face broke into a smile.

"Excuse me," I said. "I think I need to sit down for a second." I never realized how using up so much energy so fast can deplete you so entirely. I slid onto the arm of Velma's couch, and then stretched out so I was lying on the length of her couch, and the next thing I knew I was asleep, and dreaming.

Saying I Told You So

(5)

In the morning, I changed into an extra set of clothes I had at Velma's, red plaid pogo pants with a garish white hoop-studded belt, and a Julie Ruin T-shirt that said QUEEN OF THE NEIGHBORHOOD across the chest. We drove to campus to see a doctor. He put a bandage and some cotton over my knife wound and he pronounced me only lightly scraped, mostly suffering from stress and overwork. ("See?" Velma said. "I *told* you so.")

Then we climbed into Velma's car and returned to my house.

The door was shut, no sign of breakage or being forced. I turned the handle cautiously. It was unlocked.

I looked at Velma and shrugged.

Inside, the place looked normal. None of the chairs were knocked over, and the fountains of blood that I remembered had left no trace, not on the walls or the carpet or the sofa.

I rose up from the carpet, one hand on my hip. My eyes fixed on the just-ajar door that separated the living room and my bedroom. Transfixedly, as though I were still in the dream of last night, I walked, slow and determined, across the floor to my bedroom.

I pushed on the door lightly.

It swung open.

The room was dark, glowing dully through the drawn shades. My bed was unmade, not a surprise. Everything else looked undisturbed, the piles of textbooks everywhere, CDs lying on top of their cases. The flying toasters on my computer screensaver bounced around, carrying on with their usual business.

And then I saw my chair.

It lay on the ground, strewn halfway across the room from my desk, toppled on its side.

"Hey, what's that?" said Velma, her voice flooding in from the living room. I turned around and left my room. Velma stood in front of my large-screen TV, looking across the room. Her eyes fixated on a small yellow square.

Stuck to the back of the front door was a Post-It note. I took it down and read it.

i'll be back

"What does it say?" asked Velma breezily. She craned over my shoulder to see, and I tried to pull it away and fold it into my pocket before she did.

The doorknob rattled.

I gasped. I threw the note to the floor, grabbed at my belt for a gun. Why would I have a gun? I think I get all my instincts from television.

I peered into the peephole. Three men, not the same ones as last night, stood there, looking solemn. Their right hands were digging into their suit jacket pockets.

I felt my cheeks and face going red. I tried to quiet my mind, which was going crazy just then with alarm and panic and stupidity. *Control yourself, Candy Cohen,* I told myself harshly. *You are the only person who can get yourself out of this.*

Velma's breath lit my neck. She was standing right behind me. At that second I hated myself for pulling her into all this. I had managed to fight my way out, and I'd stupidly returned right back to the scene of the battle, which was bad enough. But I didn't have to get Velma into this.

I breathed deeply. Okay. I was still here. I was still a functional human being.

Now, all I had to do was get her out.

I slid the chain lock onto the door. I tried to be quiet, but I doubted it would make a difference.

"Go to the window! Now!" I hissed at Velma.

I pointed toward my open bedroom door, to the window that led to the fire escape.

Preston was climbing in through that window.

He wore a Brioni suit, jet black, cut close, and a tie so bright red that, under other circumstances, I would swear it used batteries. One arm was wrapped around the rusting metal railing of the fire escape, pulling himself up, but he looked totally chill about it, like he was lifting a teacup instead of the powerful frame of his body.

Velma stepped aside, astounded. She was quaking, and her eyes were wider than I'd ever seen them.

Preston stepped through the window frame, smoothed his hair, and began walking toward me. He unsnapped the top button of his collar and pulled down his tie.

"I wouldn't advise that neck jab you did before," he said. "I'm really tired of paralysis."

An inner collar glinted around his neck. *Glinted.* It was like steel or something.

That was the grim, cold instant when I realized just how seriously he was taking this. He was so close, I could see the muscles of his face tensing. His eyes were devoid of fear. He didn't look angry or afraid or even mildly pissed off. He just looked curious. Curious to see what I'd do next.

What did he want with me? Why did he not just leave me alone? And, why was he taking this so hardcore?

I shot out my leg.

From where I was standing, my leg—if I stretched it out straight in the air—would extend roughly two inches into his ribcage. I pulled the muscles in my knee, bending my leg in mid-kick.

Then I straightened it.

It sunk deep into his stomach. His body folded in half. The point of contact was right at his hips, the point where your body normally folds.

With the bottom of my foot, I could feel the outline of his stomach below his skin. It seized.

His body flew back into the window. It sailed straight out. His spine rattled against the fire escape as he landed, crushed and inert.

Velma stared at me, horrified.

"*Velma!*" I cried. I tugged her wrist, hard, to snap her back into reality. "Girl, look alive!"

"What is it?" Velma shook her head, dazed.

"We need to go, now!"

The front door swung open with a loud crack, the lock ripping off the wall. One of the musclemen was already saying, "Sir, do you need any—" He stopped when he saw us.

I pushed Velma through the window. I jumped out after her.

We stepped over Preston's motionless body.

And we ran.

We took the iron fire escape, two steps at a time. The stairs stopped on the second floor, ten feet above the ground. "Let's jump," I announced to Velma, stepping off the edge of the fire escape. I twisted my body as I fell. I landed on the ground in crouching position, ready to spring into a run.

I checked around me. The street was clear.

I looked up. Velma hung on, afraid to let go of the last rung of the ladder. She dangled by her small chubby fists, legs swaying in the air.

My eyes scanned the space above her. There was no sign of the goons yet.

"Velma, honey," I called. "You need to let go of the rung!"

"I don't know if I can!"

Fear splashed across her voice. I took a breath and let it out slowly.

"Okay, Velma," I said. "I want you to close your eyes."

"Okay," she said uncertainly.

"No, I mean *really* close your eyes. Not scrunching them together, not squeezing, but loose. Shut your eyes like you're going to sleep."

She didn't say anything. I could tell she was doing it.

"Now let one hand go."

She swung one arm out to the side. It shook in midair. For a second, her fingers groped at the air, then relaxed.

"Attagirl. Now, do the other on the count of—"

She dropped.

She fell straight into me. Her body knocked me over, digging my body into the concrete, plowing me flat on my ass. Velma, standing upright, offered me a hand and pulled me up.

"Where to?" she asked.

"Where's your car?" I asked. "We can't do mine. It's too risky."

Velma thought for a second. Her eyes raced. She was taking it in—not just remembering where she parked, but thinking about the night, the attack, that we were actually on the run.

She nodded left, then took off down the street, beckoning me to follow.

I did. But first I looked up at the fire escape, and what I saw—or, actually, what I didn't see—sent chills up and down my spine.

The goons weren't there.

And neither was Preston's body.

*

*   *

"Do you think Preston looked dead when we left?" I asked. I swigged a decaf lo-cal iced coffee through the green day glo straw. I must have hit ice, though, because it made one of those loud slurping sounds as if I'd tried to drink air. "Do you think I killed him?"

"Mother of God!" cried Velma. Her hands flew to her face, and the Gucci cruise dress that she'd been holding in her hands fell to the floor. "Is that even possible?"

"I'm doubting it," I said.

We were decompressing. We were trying to come down off the adrenaline high, slow our metabolisms down to a livable rate, and look normal.

We were in the Women's Casual section at the mall.

I stirred the iced coffee with the straw. This was shopping therapy at its most extreme, the two of us picking through clothes the way most people picked through leftovers.

But, oh, right, we were talking about strangulation.

"You have to have total, what do you call it, centrifugal force or something to do that. Maybe if I popped his spleen open. But, otherwise, forget it. Velms, that is *so* not your color."

Velma abruptly returned the tackily purple-and-pink ruffled dress to the display rack. She sighed, giving the dress one last moment of eye envy, and returned to her hands-on browsing. I studied the outlay of patterns carefully.

"You should call the police," Velma demurred.

My head shot up. She drained her macchiato in one long gulp.

"No, I *should* have called the police last night. Instead I fell asleep at your place. And I can just imagine the call—'Hello, I'm a college freshman. There were gangsters in my apartment. Isn't that, like, crazy?'"

"Or you could ask your father," Velma suggested, turning slightly red. Ever since he'd started coming over every Saturday, treating her grandparents and the poodles, she'd always had a kind of adolescent crush on my father.

I shook my head adamantly. "God, Velma. You *need* to get off this my-father kick. And besides—I can't. It would just give him a heart attack."

Velma shrugged. She wanted to argue, but there was no way.

"How about this one?" I asked, pulling a new Betsey Johnson off the rack with my one free hand.

I held it against her. The dress was a simple olive number, short sleeves, normal neckline, one seam at the waist with white piping on the edges. But the exact light brown color blended with Velma's adorable freckles and her perpetually confused look. It made her look simple and sultry, like a fairy-tale princess; just holding it up against her, it brought out more Velma than most of the conversations she'd ever had. Velma always tried to put people at ease, and she wound up losing herself in the process.

But this dress, it really did her good.

"I don't know," Velma said, twisting the thin fabric in her hands. "Do you think it'll do enough for my hips?"

There was a sound of clumping footsteps, like someone walking fast and trying not to run. We both looked over. It was a mall security guard.

"Excuse me, ladies." He walked over to us. One hand rested on his belt.

"Yes?" I said, trying to keep my voice steady.

"We seem to have a situation, and I'm wondering if you could help us out."

He kept advancing, kept walking toward us.

There was something funny about him. I could tell that right off. Most security guards in most malls, they're fat and lazy and they drift through the mall thinking their own thoughts every day like a routine.

Velma squeezed my forearm.

The teen-pop music in the store was loud, louder than usual, and it filled my head with all the lame lyrics that I knew by heart even though I never wanted to. I thought he was asking if he could help us, *Is there a problem?* But it came out sounding like *Do you have a problem?* And then his hand was on his holster, fingers toying with his billy club, and his lips were moving and it seemed like he was trying to take me in, when it hit me.

He was not acting at all like mall security guards were supposed to act.

"Do you—" his voice warbled. He sounded nervous. Was he nervous? "Do either of you know who Candace Cohen, known to acquaintances as Candy, is? She's known to frequent this mall, and her profile says that she's about your age. We've got some questions for her."

I swallowed.

Velma's eyes got wide. Her hand moved from my forearm to my hand, and she squeezed tight.

"Oh my God," she said.

My fingers twitched, long and stiff. Covertly, I folded them into a White Stork grip—fingers together, knuckles spread apart—ready to swing up my hand and peck his eyes out.

"Portia!" Velma exclaimed. "You remember Candy Cohen? She was at that party last week. She is such. A. Bitch." Velma folded her other hand delicately over her chest, turned to the guard, and made her eyes go even wider. "Begging your pardon for the indecent language, sir, but she's a friend of a friend of an acquaintance of mine, you understand. My friend had the most *devas*tating crush on the most devastating boy, and he was all over Candy, and, oh, I must have been so weak-willed— most of us girls just *get* like that, I suppose, although I do try to suppress it whilst I can—and I just wanted to absolutely *mur*der her." Velma barked out a curdling twitter of a laugh. "Not in that arrestable way, I mean."

The poor old-man security guard—who, come to think of it, looked a lot like Velma's grandfather, only in a security-guard uniform—looked *so* fiercely apologetic.

I shook my head, *forget it*, not even trying to explain.

As naturally as possible, we switched sections, walking across the store. We left the guard looking baffled and apologetic, scratching his head beneath his security-guard visor, and crossed the store as fast as we could.

"Okay, that's it," I hissed in Velma's ear, storming through the bargain racks. "I'm doing it. I'm calling 9-1-1."

Velma got this horrified look on her face and shook her head vehemently. But I was over it. There are some people who like not being in the driver's seat, and I was not one of them. Like, there were all these crazy things that were never supposed to happen to anyone, and now they were happening to me. If those were all straws, this was the absolute last one.

I picked up my cell phone and dialed. "9-1-1," said the operator right away. "Can I have your current location?"

"I'd like to report an emergency," I began.

"First off, we need to know your location, please, ma'am."

"Why do you need to know where I'm at?"

Velma cut the air with her hands, signaling *no* even harder. "Give them my grandparents' address," she mouthed the words at me.

"Standard procedure. In any emergency, we dispatch the nearest police officers."

"Alright, I'm at 110 East Hartford in Mansour."

I could hear her typing it in. "And what's your name?"

"Candace Bettina Cohen."

"And what is the nature of your emergency?"

"I'd like to report a . . . stalker," I said. Was that the word for it?

I bit my lip and looked around the mall. Young girls sitting on the fountain ledge, mothers schlepping around their bratty kids. In the meantime, Velma had picked up her own cell phone. She was using that docile, obedient voice that she only used with her grandmother.

"Yes, yes, sure I'll hold on, Grandma," Velma was saying. "No, I *am* doing fine." She listened for a minute. "Yes, that *is* odd. Were you expecting anyone? . . . Well, I don't know, I might have told someone to stop by. Is it a police car? No, it isn't, it's a limo." She lowered the phone and mouthed to me, "Limo!" Then she cleared her throat and resumed talking in a normal voice. "No, I wouldn't know what to tell them. Listen, Grandma, I might be going away for a few weeks. I don't know where, but of course I'll let you know when I do. Now go answer the door. I love you." She hung up.

I stared at my own phone, the one I'd just said her grandmother's address into, and clicked off in horror.

"A limo?" I asked.

Velma nodded grimly.

"He's good," she said. "That just means we have to be better."

She removed another cell phone from her bag, one that I didn't recognize. It looked smaller, slicker, something like more *aerodynamic*. If phones could fly, this one would break the sound barrier. Also, you know how most phones are silver, not actual silver but painted silver? This phone was gold.

She flipped it open, turned the power on, and dialed memory-1.

"Velma, what is up with that?" I said. "Why am I not memory-1?"

"*Shut up.*"

The voice that came out of Velma's mouth just then was not one that I'd ever heard. I don't mean literally, like she started talking like a demon beast or anything, but the transition was almost that seamless. She barked orders. She asked questions that were quick and concise. When whoever was on the other line didn't have an answer for Velma—or an answer she liked—she let loose on them. This, from a girl who normally asks permission before hanging up on her boyfriend.

"Okay," Velma hung up. "We can't go to New York. The reservation is in your name. He's sure to have people watching that plane."

"Oh my God!" I gasped. I'd totally forgotten about catching the plane. I pulled out my cell, finger on the trigger to call Matty.

Her hand clamped down before I could hit the SEND button. "Don't."

"So we'll catch another plane. New York's a big city."

Velma flashed me a look. "We can't risk it. He probably knows where Matty lives, and he'll be watching for us there. My security director says we should avoid New York at all costs. We should lie low, take precautions, and move often and fast." She hit another memory key, which was also in the top row and it was also not my number.

"Who are you calling now? And for God's sake, Velma, since when do you have a security director?"

"You *know* him, Candy. It's Mr. Patterson."

"But you always said Mr. Patterson was your travel agent."

"Well, you can't just *ad*vertise your family secrets to the world, can you? I thought you'd figured it out by now—hold on, here he is." She swung the cell phone open again.

I felt awful. My head was spinning, I was feeling more out of control than ever, and worst of all, I'd totally forgotten that I was going to go visit Matty. The one simple, unadulterated non-sucky thing in my life, and it had slipped my mind. Maybe it was better that I wasn't going to get to see him. Maybe, if we ever really *did* hang out and if we ever really *did* go on a date, I would wind up being the most awful, irresponsible girlfriend ever. Being as though I already pretty much was. The awful and irresponsible part, at least.

Velma hung up and looked at me exasperatedly. "I *swear*. I have to kick *every*one's ass before they'll do one simple identity transfer for me."

"What family secrets are you talking about?"

"That, you know. That my family is Family."

"You mean, like—*Sopranos* family?"

"*Eww.* Maybe if we lived in New Jersey and had no decent hairstylists. But come *on*, C.B., I thought you knew."

"You never *told* me."

"Well, you never told me that you had problems with commitment from the premature death of your mother, but I figured *that* out on my own, didn't I?"

"Jesus." I bit my lip. *I* hadn't even completely figured that out yet.

I felt the cold, distant dread spring out of my head, replaced by the immediate worry that Preston's men were already on our tail. "Fine, then," I agreed. "Let's do what they tell us. Where are we flying to?"

"Somewhere special," said Velma. "But we're flying there from Washington."

"But what about my classes?"

"Forget your classes, Candy! They had guns."

"Okay," I said, huffing through pursed lips. "But I'm bringing my textbooks."

Mr. Patterson told us to hang out downtown, walk around the blocks in very slow, random patterns. When we passed the big Macy's on Peachtree Street, he said to walk inside the building and come out another exit. For maybe the first time ever, neither Velma nor I felt like lingering.

Finally on the middle of Peachtree, a car pulled up beside us, slowed down for a few minutes. I looked at Velma. She nodded that it was okay, she recognized them, and we slid into the back seat during the brief second of a red light. The window up front rolled down, and a buzz-cut driver turned to wave to us.

"Hello," he said. His voice was a low baritone, almost deeper than human ears could understand. He nodded cordially to me, and then, more familiarly at Velma. "We're driving to Reagan National Airport?"

"That's correct," said Velma.

"Your attaché bags are in the trunk. Have a pleasant ride."

The window rolled back up.

That was the last we saw of him for nine hours. We kicked off our shoes, put our feet on the seats, and pretended that this was an airplane going to France: posh interiors, cheesy low-alcohol alcoholic drinks (there were wine spritzers in the micro-fridge), and sucky in-flight radio. We listened to the country station all the way to the North Carolina border. It drove us mad, but it got a few nervous giggles out of us that we really needed to have. On the way out of Atlanta, I asked Velma whether it was safe to call Matty. She flicked open her other phone, the mysterious one, and nodded. "We're still on the Atlanta calling towers," she said. "You have five minutes, maybe seven."

She handed me the phone. I pulled out that Steaks & Co. cocktail napkin and typed in the number I'd been carrying in my purse all week. Halfway through entering it, Matty's full name popped up onscreen.

I looked up at Velma. "This phone knows his number?"

Velma looked uninterested. "That phone knows everybody's number."

Matty's line picked up on the first ring. There was a brief pause, and then a small voice, high and wavery and uncertain, came out. "H-hello?"

"Hello," I said, collected and businesslike. "May I please speak to Matty, if he is available?"

"This is he. Who are you?"

"Do you get that many calls from strange girls whose voices you don't recognize?" I asked, and my voice softened. It's weird how you become so aware of these things, once your voice is all you have to work with.

"Naw. Most of the strange girls, I recognize their voices straight off."

"Nice."

"Not half as nice as it'll be in an hour. Are you guys already in the air?"

I paused. Suddenly, the rush hit me. Not only did he have no idea about the situation, he had no idea about anything.

"We're . . ."

"You're not coming."

"We *are* coming. It's just that, there's been an accident."

There was silence from his end for a second. "Oh no. Are you okay? Is Velma?"

"We're fine, Matty. It's not that. It's just . . ."

The phone let out a beep.

Velma looked up. "Get off!" she said, all Girl Scout Leader again.

"Well, things are complicated. But I have to go. I'll call you again when I can?"

"In other words, not soon enough."

"Get off the line!" Velma hissed.

"Bingo, kiddo." I hung up.

The first thing she did, Velma reached over and checked the display. There were little meters all over the phone in red and green, electronic gauges for I don't even know what. She nodded, satisfied. "Eighteen seconds to spare," she said. "Nice."

"Eighteen seconds?" I asked. "You're that anal?"

"I'm hard-ass because I care." Velma smiled at me, tossed the phone in her purse, and rolled into a ball on the backseat.

I watched the land fly by. Grassy hills grew to mountains, creeks wound with the steep turns in the road. The land stretched out for miles, vacant, with country houses dotting the empty landscape like stray darts. I wondered what it would be like to live out there. Nobody around for a million miles. I wondered what they did for fun at night. Maybe turned off all the lights so there was no light coming from anywhere.

I slept. My dreams were crazy and vivid, and I woke up in a cold sweat. I sat up suddenly and the car was dark, an unfamiliar suit jacket draped over me like a blanket. My hair stuck to my face and as I brushed it out, it felt like walking through hippie beads hung over the kitchen doorway at a college party.

"What's wrong, Candy?" Velma peered at me through the dark. She was sitting straight up in her seat, staring out the window. "What were you dreaming about?"

I blinked at her sleepily. Through the whole ride, she hadn't slept at all, I was sure. Velma was my guardian angel, I decided groggily. I didn't know what I would ever do without her.

I grunted, shaking my head. "Nothing," I felt myself mutter, although my mouth was hoarse and no noises came out. The long horizon was gray, almost black. The day had sunk into nothing. In a flash of sudden, inspirational hopelessness, it occurred to me that every single thing I'd thought would come true today hadn't.

At least we were almost at the airport.

My Best Friend's Secret

(6)

We hopped a quick series of flights, D.C. to Phoenix to Boston to Iowa City. In Iowa City, we waited for four and a half hours, missing one flight before buying tickets for the next one ten minutes before the boarding call came. I swallowed the world's biggest sigh of anxiety, watching Velma click her nail placidly on the board marked DEPARTURES. "I understand why we're hopping around the country," I said, "but why are we intentionally missing our flights? Doesn't that defeat the purpose of, I don't know, running?"

"To stay on top of the chase," Velma told me in a lecturey voice. "Mr. Patterson says, as long as we're being unexpected, we're doing what we're supposed to."

I hated Mr. Patterson. I wanted to be home, going crazy because of little stupid things like pimples and boys, things that I could turn off if I wanted. Failing that, I wanted to be naked on a beach drinking alcoholic drinks that had colors instead of flavors.

"Well, can't we run to Bermuda, then?" I kvetched.

"No passports. Mr. Patterson says, the less paper-work we use, the safer we are."

"I think Mr. Patterson is a little too OCD for his own good."

"He's paranoid, Candy," Velma pursed her lips. "That's why he's the director of security and we're not."

I folded my arms crossly. "So, where to next?"

Traces of a smile crept across Velma's lips.

"That would be telling," she said, stepping backwards away from me. She raised a credit card to her lips, the magic one whose numbers kept changing. "Stay here and try not to get in too much trouble. I'll be back."

I stayed looking annoyed until Velma vanished in the direction of the ticket counters. Then I spun around, hands behind my back, looking innocent—and really being innocent, too, until the very single moment my eyes hit the wall of internet terminals.

"candy!"

"Matty?"

"hey, what's up? where are you???"

"Uh . . . Europe, maybe?"

"i won't even ask."

"Thanks. Listen, I'm sorry I keep flaking out. It's just . . ."

"no, you don't even have to say. i mean, i under-stand. i'm so there."

"You *are*?"

"sure. work. velma told me, you're a model, you must get tons of these last-minute photo shoots. the magazine business has been crazy lately, i've been clocking double shifts every day this week. it's been, like, pure agony—by the time i get out, it's practically dead dark outside."

A sudden shiver. "Matty—don't say dead, okay?"

"sorry. it was just an expression. besides, i thought models only got superstitious about cut roses and stuff."

"It's not superstition. It's just . . ."

"yeah?"

"You're my good-luck charm. Just don't say dead."

"ok. but, candy. you know what?"

"What?"

"when you *do* get here, you'd better use that model money to take me out in style."

I was just getting off when Velma ran up to me, breathless, two tickets in her hand. I thought she was going to rush me off to another block-long line, but when she saw where I was coming from, she froze.

"What. Did. You. Just. Do."

"I was just talking to Matty, it was no big deal—"

"Candy. *You went on the internet?*"

I felt this sudden pit of anxiety in my stomach, the way I used to when it was six o'clock and I hadn't done my homework yet and my mother suddenly went all screaming and ballistic on me.

"I told you, it was nothing. All I did was go on the website, it was anonymous, they don't even have my real *name*—"

"And how did you pay for that internet access?"

Now it was my turn to get clammy and neurotic. My fingers tightened around my purse.

The purse that had my credit card in it.

"Velma, I'm sorry."

I got a swallow lodged in my throat and my protests, my apologies, they all got stuck. Letting down that stodgy old Mr. Patterson was one thing, but letting down Velma was another. And I didn't even get to talk to my father, just some boy.

"It's no big deal," she said. She dropped her carry-on bag, walked over to the row of padded plastic chairs, and sank into one. "We'll just put up another smokescreen. There's always the red-eye flight, I suppose."

*

* *

San Francisco that morning was cold and damp, the opposite of the way winter is supposed to be in California. Not harsh, only disagreeable. I still wasn't happy. I was feeling for the first time like a true spoiled brat, the exact attitude I was slaving away at the burger joint to shrug off, feeling like I would spend every penny of my inheritance to erase this whole mess and be back home. I wanted Atlanta, where the only sign that it was winter was the jokes old men were cracking about importing penguins into New York when it snowed too much.

New York. I'd just bought the best winter coat, three different kinds of fake fur lining. It was the warmest thing you'd ever felt, and still revealing enough so you didn't look like a gorilla. I was so excited for New York that I wasn't even going to mind the cold.

But most of my clothes were three thousand miles away now.

I was a wanted girl. These were the sacrifices I had to make.

Another nameless, formless car dragged us from the airport to downtown San Francisco. We kept the tinted windows up, but you could still feel the tilt of the car, riding up hills, swiveling around sudden street corners.

I rolled down the window the tiniest bit. Velma shot me a look, but I didn't care. I inhaled. My lungs filled up with salty fresh air. It even tasted green. I watched the trees drift past my window, one after the other in a line, and it felt like an old-fashioned parade, even if we were zooming in total secrecy toward a totally random hotel on a street with a zillion other hotels on an anonymous block of downtown San Francisco.

This was the plan: word had leaked from high up in Velma's Family—oh, okay, the *Mafia,* I said it—that, not only was Preston after me, but he had also involved Velma, and their job, above everything else, was to protect Velma. They could do that. They could do anything.

Which is why, right now, we were being swept away, off the face of the earth. Protected. Hidden. Untraceable.

The firm black second-hand-of-a-Patek-watch-like bristles of my appliqué brush swooshed down hard, swiped a single bright pink streak across the brim of my leftmost toe, the teeniest toenail of all. It struck, splashed a bright, sudden swatch of color, then pulled away with an air of finality, retreating back into the polish bottle. I pulled it close to investigate, contemplated, and, satisfied, gave it a quick series of three brief-but-controlled breaths.

Late morning, and the sun was coming out.

Life wasn't good, but it could be worse.

A shadow fell over me. Instinctively, I reached up to my neck and tugged up the cleavage line of my bikini top.

Velma peered down at me.

"Okay," she said, "I just got off the phone with Mr. Patterson, and it's like this."

I grimaced. "Hit me."

"They said to stay here."

"On the beach? I think I can take this kind of imprisonment." I flopped back onto the beach towel, letting my naked arms crash into the small dales of sand and shells that the wind had piled around me.

Velma planted herself on the edge of the blanket and crossed her legs. "Mr. Patterson says that it will take your, um, employer—" she coughed, "—he says that it'll take Preston a few days to figure out where we've vanished to. And by then, hopefully, they can broker a deal with the Reign people."

"A deal?"

Velma looked uncomfortable. "They'll arrange some sort of peace treaty between families. My Family will give him something he really wants, and he'll stop hunting us."

"You mean, me."

"Us." Velma squeezed my hand.

I pulled it away. "But what will you have to give up? Will it be something valuable?"

"No, not at all. Probably just some piece of land they've been fighting over or something," said Velma. But she looked unsure.

When the sun finally receded enough to make tanning a completely untenable option, we made our way to the Castro, the shopping district. Mr. Patterson had warned us about a zillion times to lay low, not go to any dance clubs or fancy restaurants or do anything that might call undue attention to ourselves, but we were pretty sure he only meant in the straight world.

Straight girls never feel as safe as they do among gay men. It's a strange thing, because it's like hanging out with your bitchiest female friend in the world, only for some reason it's not as obnoxious. Probably because it allows straight girls to be catty without the worry of being judged. Plus the gay men who know couture are practically, like, style *gods*. They know women's fashion better than almost any woman. And gay chic is always the chicest chic of all.

On top of that, gay men are such drama queens that, next to them, straight women are practically low-maintenance.

With that in mind, we hit the stores on 18th and Castro.

Velma and I tried to lay low. We only looked at the merchandise on display and didn't even try to persuade our way into the stock rooms. Velma went as far as to shoot an admonishing look in my direction when I picked out a flashy red dress that was half sequins and half non-existent. "We *need* to lay *LOW*," she mouthed at me.

I shrugged. At least the designer was local.

We bought power smoothies in an internet café, and while Velma was off in the bathroom, I handed the cashier a twenty-dollar bill and hooked myself up with some anonymous internet access.

Matty was on, of course. "Don't you ever do anything else with your life?" I typed to him.

"you mean, besides waiting for you to come online? never," he replied.

"Now that's my kind of man."

"i think it would be cool to be a househusband. you know, to do my chores and wait around for my girl to come home and . . ."

"And what?" I prompted him.

"you know. i'd be like a kitchen appliance. always ready. ;)"

"Be careful what you wish for. I've been compared to rabbits."

"are you always in this kind of mood?"

"I'm *never* in this kind of mood."

"really?"

"Not really. But I never let anyone else know when I feel like this."

"well, tell me about something else. when can i see you?"

"As soon as we get outta here. I promise."

"so how is san francisco, anyway?"

My fingers froze on the keys.

Calmly, trying not to show anyone in the café any sign of panic, I moved my mouse pointer up to the *close* button. As my finger went down, Matty sent another message: "wait!"

"Explain yourself QUICK."

"i'm sorry!!! i really really really did not mean to freak you out."

"Matty, I should go."

"all i did was read your DNS protocol."

"My what?"

"i swear. it's easy to do, and it only works when you're actually net-talking to me. i promise not to do it again. i'm not spying. i'm just being too curious. and a little. bit. jealous."

"Jealous? Of what?"

"i keep thinking the reason you're not coming to see me is cause you're off having another rendezvous with one of your super power society friends. so when i know you're just in san francisco and you're looking me up anyway, it all starts getting a little more okay."

Jealous. Jealous was okay. I could handle jealous.

I jumped offline a second before Velma came back, swinging her bag, fixing her hair the way that you do when you've already fixed your hair but feel like something's still out of place.

That's how I'd been feeling about Matty all week.

Like everything was perfect, so perfect it hurt, but there was still something wrong.

The trouble with being in hiding is, there's almost no way to do it well. I mean, the less you *do*, the better in hiding you are. And I'm practically the worst person in the world at doing nothing.

Valencia Street was one ten-minute cab ride away, but it was all the way on the far side of town, and after the Castro, Velma was feeling jumpy. After five o'clock, when the businesses let out and the tourists all vanished back inside their hotels to develop film or clean out their fanny packs or whatever it is that normal tourists do, we retreated to the Fairmont to freshen up and plan our next move. Mr. Patterson had said to keep a low profile, and so we spent the rest of the afternoon in the hotel's tanning salon, and then in our room, taking showers and breezing through the local literature—that is, in the form of magazines and cable TV.

I flipped my magazine shut. The last page of magazines, where they have fashion don'ts or the amusing story or the readers' poll, was usually my favorite part, but there was this big picture of me on the inside back cover, staring at the camera all enthusiastically bored. That was probably the exact way I looked right now. If it was, I hoped nobody was looking at me.

"Velma?" I said.

Velma looked up from the book she was reading, *Bartleby the Scrivener* or something. It was totally *not* airport reading, totally defeating our undercover tourist-ness. But that was Velma for you.

"Yeah?"

"What do you say we go grab a drink?"

The hotel bar was perfect for our purposes. Ten dollars for a beer was too ludicrously expensive for anyone, even the tourists who stayed here, and at a ten-dollar-a-beer bar, they were *so* never going to ID us. The décor took the worst parts of the Prohibition and synth-pop eras and molded them into a kind of futuristic-looking place that nobody would feel comfortable in, and also, there had to be at least a dozen bars within a two-block radius that served better drinks for cheaper, and all probably had historical significance, too, leaving this place basically empty. That was good for us.

We ordered cosmopolitans. They came with umbrellas. That was how top-of-the-line geekwad this bar was. Taking care to keep our white shirts far, far away from the rims of our glasses, we huddled over the table and talked shop.

"Okay, wait," I said to Velma. "This is what I don't understand. If we have the mob on our side, why can't they just, like, give him a pair of cement shoes and make him walk with the fishes?"

"They don't *do* that," Velma said petulantly. She beat at her drink with the little plastic umbrella. "They're the Mafia, not Dr. Dre."

"Whatever it is they do, then. Why can't they just do it?"

"Oh, Candy. You don't understand. I hope you never understand these things."

I hit the bar with my palms. "I hate when you treat me like that! Velma—*Jesus*—I'm premed. I think I can handle the choreography of hired goons hitting people over the head."

"Then imagine," Velma said, calmly and placidly, "that there isn't just one set of hired goons hitting other people over the head."

"Oh."

"Yeah."

"You mean this guy—Preston—has his own goons?"

"We don't exactly call them *goons*. But, otherwise, yes. Preston, in his own way, is very powerful."

"And not just in the field of women's underwear."

"Look," said Velma. "That's your industry. I'm not making any judgments about *that* . . . ."

Suddenly, I felt the barest flush of wind on my spine. My face heated up. It was that almost-invisible radiation that you feel when someone's gaze is fixed on you. When you know somebody's watching.

I lowered my drink from my lips. "Velma," I said. "I have this horrible feeling someone's watching us."

"People are always watching you. Guys, anyway."

"No, but this is different." I reached into my purse, fished something out, and snapped it shut. "I don't want to turn around. Can you see anyone who looks suspicious?"

"Nobody looks—"

"Oh, come on. Be a little less trusting. Is anyone eyeing us weirdly?"

Velma bit her lip. I could see the hesitation in her eyes. "There's a guy in pleated khakis who's working on a laptop and staring at your ass. A family of four finishing up dinner. The woman keeps looking in our direction, but there are kids. There's—okay, this might be something—two guys in their thirties, they look like they just got off work, but there's something about them. They don't look like they're just talking business. My grandparents' friends never look that casual when they're talking business."

"Go on."

"I don't know. They look discerning—almost hostile— but not hostile toward each other. Okay, the family is definitely putting on their coats, it's not them. These guys, it's not like they're negotiating or talking about a boss they hate. They're just *waiting*. They—"

"Tell me what they do now."

I stood up and turned around casually, as though I were going to the bathroom. My eyes swept over them too fast to see anything. I left my purse on my chair. I moved slowly, one hand on the bar. I never took my eyes off Velma.

"One of the guys just pulled on his coat. He looks like he's going to follow you."

I dropped the bill I'd taken from my purse on the counter and, in the same move, swept the purse into my arm. "Let's go," I said.

We walked nonchalantly away from the bar, toward the ladies' room, and then at the last second I punched the elevator call button for the hotel's back elevators. Out of the corner of my eye, I saw the two guys from the bar turn the corner. At that moment, a waiter emerged from the kitchen, breezing past us and preventing the guys from breaking into obvious pursuit. Velma managed to snatch a kumquat from the waiter's tray. I just shook my head at her. As she popped it into her mouth, her expression said, *What?*

Suddenly, with a delicate ping, and before the waiter realized what happened with the dessert, the doors in front of us slid open. I discreetly pushed Velma in. I was hoping the two guys would head to our floor, thinking we were going back to our room. Velma randomly pressed the third floor button and looked at me.

"Okay, we just get off at whatever floor, and go back downstairs and exit out the front door. They'll never expect that," I said, desperately hoping that she believed me.

She nodded as the doors opened to the third floor. "We don't have time to wait for the elevator again. Our room was only on the eighteenth floor." Velma darted out of the elevator, almost knocking over an older woman. We called out apologies and raced for the stair-case entrance.

Shoving open the NO RE-ENTRY ON THIS FLOOR door, we dashed down the stairs. It was dangerous going with our heels, but there was no time to stop.

We exploded out of the stairwell and tumbled into the lobby, still moving at full speed. Without bothering to slow down, we ran toward the entrance, pausing only for the large glass revolving door.

Once out on the street we ducked into an alley a few buildings down.

"What next?" I asked Velma, panting for air beside me.

"Next?" said Velma, as though I was ridiculous for even asking. "Next, we keep running."

We were back on the street. In front of us was a big brick wall. To the right was uphill. To the left was down, a bunch of office buildings in the distance. Flags and building signs in wavy paintbrush script flew in the foreground.

It was Chinese writing. We were in Chinatown.

Velma pulled out her gold phone as we ran. She held it to her ear and yelled instructions without even dialing. She was so slick.

"Patterson!" she yelled. Our heels clicked against the pavement. I decided I was impressed how she ordered people around by their last names when she got agitated. "We need an out!"

Buildings flew by as though we were on bikes. Running downhill was always such a rush. Besides that, you could run faster, which was the reason I turned downhill.

I pivoted around with one foot. Velma snapped her phone shut.

"Velma!" I pulled her around the corner.

The street sloped drastically. I caught Velma before she toppled down. We ran down the street, twisted around the first corner we found, and vanished. I turned, just enough to see the two guys stuck on the corner up the street, craning their necks, scratching their balding heads.

"We're good," I said.

"Not for long," said Velma. "They'll figure it out. Mr. Patterson says to walk thirty steps south and wait."

"Which way is south?" I said.

Velma brought her phone out again. The antenna swung left and pointed down the alley.

We walked quickly. Velma counted, but she was too shaken, she kept speaking out loud. When we got to twenty-seven (or was it twenty-eight?), an old, shrunken Chinese man in a white apron appeared two storefronts down, holding a bag of fortune cookies bigger than his head. He glared at us when he saw us.

"Thirty steps!" he hissed, waving us to follow him. "Thirty!"

"We're sorry," said Velma. "I thought it was—"

"Come!" He vanished inside a door.

I looked at Velma. She nodded confirmation.

We followed him. Above the door hung a sign, SAN FRANCISCO FORTUNE COOKIE COMPANY. Inside, five or six old Chinese men in white smocks stained with streaks of fortune-cookie beige and brown sat around huge, rusting machines, relics of the Iron Age. The machines popped out hot little cookie discs, and the old men grabbed handfuls of little paper fortunes and folded them inside, pulling the cookies shut with fast, confident thumb scrunches.

Our guide whistled, and a mob of thirty five-year-old kids popped up from nowhere and formed a chaotic crowd around the entrance, screaming and yelping. The man beckoned us to follow him through the labyrinth of machine-laced tunnel running back into the shadows of the factory.

We went through one door, then another, and wound through a passageway made of bamboo and wood. Along the way, our feet crunched the shattered skeletons of fortune cookies from ages past. I thought of the time Velma and I had gone to Egypt and the Prime Minister's son took us into these catacombs and we pretended to be Indiana Jones. The Prime Minister's son had flashed us dirty looks, but we ignored him.

We emerged into the back of a Chinese boutique, one of those stores that sold every unmentionably cheap, gaudy item known to humanity, crowded with fart bombs and wall calendars and bags of XXX fortune cookies and lame San Francisco tourist postcards and T-shirts.

The old man looked around and whistled. Immediately, an even older woman emerged from behind a stack of hooded sweatshirts. She was dressed in a blue kimono, hair pulled back in a tight bun. She maneuvered her way around the store like she owned it, which she probably did. The two of them talked for a minute in Mandarin Chinese, glancing back at us several times. Velma picked up a plastic number puzzle off a display rack and began to fiddle with it. She solved it in about thirty seconds, the exact time it took for them to decide what to do with us. I told you Velma was smart.

The woman waddled over to a clothes rack. She rifled through piles for a second, pulled out two handfuls of clothes, and shoved them into our arms. She pointed at the door we'd just come through—"Private room," she told us. "Change into these."

Velma and I eyed the proffered clothes like they were death incarnate. "Um, these are *tourist* clothes," I said. "We can't wear these." It was true. They were more than cheesy—they were gaudy. One of the shirts said ALCATRAZ in big university letters. The other one said WELCOME TO SAN FRANCISCO! NOW, GO HOME. Beneath them were tucked-in Bermuda shorts. With outfits like that, simply no one would believe we were staying in San Francisco's most exclusive hotel.

"I thought they were running from gangsters?" the old woman asked the old man, in Mandarin.

"We are," answered Velma, also in Mandarin. "But we cannot afford to look suspicious."

The old man and the old woman shot glances at each other.

Ten minutes later, we were on the street, Velma in a designer kimono with a flowing silk skirt beneath it, me in a red satin high-necked shirt with a pattern of flying golden dragons that came down to thigh-length and was passable as a minidress on me. Velma wrapped her hair in a matching scarf, and mine, which had been down all the way, spread over my back, was now tucked tightly under a chin-length jet-black wig. The old Chinese woman had done our makeup in the complete darkness of the secret passage, and when we emerged, she led us to the novelty mirror aisle, where you could buy mirrors that looked like your face on the cover of *Time* magazine. We stared at our faces in the compact red-rimmed reflection. We looked like different people.

We weaved quickly through the crowd down the main street of Chinatown. Beside me, Velma spoke on the phone with Mr. Patterson in Mandarin. She said it was just in case anybody important was overhearing. There was no chance they would understand Mandarin, not unless Preston and his armies had deliberately prepared for that. And, also, it came off as sounding natural in the center of Chinatown. Especially when the only people listening were the white, middle-American tourists.

Well, the old skeezy Mr. Patterson might be fluent in Mandarin, but I wasn't. I followed Velma in a huff, resenting that I didn't understand anything being said, and when I tried to go off on my own—to examine teas in a tea shop or sort through DVDs in one of the zillion bootleg vendors—Velma instantly grabbed my wrist and carted me along like a child.

Yeah, like a child. I was beginning to feel like a child, being lectured and told where to go and when I could speak to my friends and how not to get killed.

Just when I was about to pitch a tantrum for real, Velma got off the phone and tucked it into the folds of her kimono. "Okay, we can't stay here," she said. "Mr. Patterson is going to have someone get our luggage from our rooms, and we'll leave in the morning."

"But we can't stay there tonight, can we?" I said. "They'll know where we are."

"No, we can't," said Velma, and then shut her mouth.

I was going to ask her what the plan was, when suddenly, I shut mine too.

Our pursuers were walking down the street.

They passed us cleanly, not stopping or saying a word. I felt one of them sweeping his gaze over the crowd, head to head, lingering on me, passing quickly from my face and fixating on my chest. I almost wanted to laugh, but I bit the inside of my lip until they were out of earshot.

Velma let out a deep sigh. "Okay, so we can't stay here," she said. "And, yeah, we can't stay in a hotel. They know where we're staying, and they know where we *would* stay as an alternative."

"So what's the alternative to the alternative?"

"Mr. Patterson said we don't have to do this." Velma looked uncomfortable. "But he also said it's the surest way for them not to find us."

"What is it?"

"It's the last place on earth that Preston would look for you," said Velma. Nervously, she twisted the phone antenna into spirals around her finger.

We sat by a raging fire that jumped against the black metal grill. The grill probably had the remains of hamburgers and dirt and lord *knows* what kind of germs on it, but Velma insisted that we behave like normal campers, out on a normal camping trip.

I shuddered, thinking of how many normal campers used normal toilet paper without washing their normal hands afterward.

The fire sizzled as it touched cool air, and Velma jumped back in shock. She looked at me like I was crazy, sitting on the air mattress, watching the fire indifferently. She thought I was being distant, but I wasn't. My brain was going at full speed. I just didn't know how to let it out through my mouth.

Our tent was pitched behind us, in an enclave with our campfire and bags. We'd taken a cab to the ocean on the outskirts of the city, then taken another cab three miles south, then walked another mile up. The pedometer on Velma's phone (her regular phone, not the golden one) told us when the mile was up. We found a tent, sleeping bags, and new clothes just where Mr. Patterson said we would, under a large rock that rolled right over when you pushed on the right depression.

Soy dogs and skewers were included in the cooler, which was buried in the sand, even a genuine real-meat hamburger for Velma. What was not included was a fire. It was a good thing I'd brought enough nail polish remover to serve as lighter fluid, or else I don't know what we would've done.

We sat by the fire, gleaning a slow warmth.

"Are you doing okay?" Velma asked.

"No, actually," I said. "I'm actually not doing okay. More than anything else, I'm feeling pissed off about this whole thing. All I wanted to do was be in New York, and I *know* I'm spoiled, that's not what it is at all. I mean, I'm used to getting what I want, but it just seems so unfair that I want this thing—and there's about a million things standing in between us—and it's not even things that are *supposed* to be there. He wants to see me. I want to see him. But I have this day job that I didn't even ap*ply* for that just won't let go of me. And you know what, Velm? The benefits package sucks. It really absolutely sucks."

"Wow," said Velma.

She really sounded wowed. As though she was impressed with me or something.

"What?" I demanded, annoyed at her bright-eyed-ness.

"You're going through this much bad stuff," she said, "and what you're most upset about is meeting Matty."

I tapped the sticky, watery sand with one toe of my strappy sandals.

"That," said Velma, "is the most positive thing I've ever heard."

We slept that night on Ocean Beach, and in the morning we were awakened by the hippies who had been sleeping downstream from us, scuffling and gathering their things before the morning policemen came to clear us off. Mr. Patterson had instructed us to be gone by daybreak, even though the first cruiser of the morning didn't usually come through until 7:30 A.M.

And in that murky gray morning, Velma somehow made friends with the hippies—people who were dirty and despised showers, disliked genetically modified foods, and had hairstyles that it had *never* been socially acceptable for white people to have—and they offered to drive us to the airport in their Mystery Machine van, replete with a pull-out double bed and a sink that sprayed beer from the faucet. Velma offered to let them keep our tent and provisions if they didn't tell anyone they'd met us. "Puh-*leeze,*" the girl driving the van said. "Like we'd tell the pigs anything in the first place?" We all laughed, although from Velma and me, it felt a bit forced. Not like they could tell. They probably thought that everything we did was forced.

"So," I asked Velma, "do you have our tickets?"

"This time," she said, "we don't need tickets."

"Where are we going, then?"

"Even if I knew, I couldn't tell you."

We took a private jet. Flying on private planes was cool, but it didn't actually feel like flying—no stewardesses, no in-flight snack, and no odd people walking past your seat and checking you out. But once you get off, you're right back in the airport and it always still *feels* like an airport, pedestrian families with whiny children, floors like dried bubblegum.

Except this time.

The doors swung open, the pilot let us out, and suddenly we were standing in a mahogany office. My heels touched down onto the plush bounce of fresh carpet, and the smallness of the room swallowed the plane into the background.

There was a filing cabinet and a desk. There was a bearskin rug, a micro-fridge, and a tumbler of brown liquid with glasses resting atop it. A WWF-sized bald man with a brisk goatee stood behind the desk, silent and tough, with his hands clasped in front of his belt.

A cute, warm-looking guy a few years older than us—well, okay, maybe ten years older, but a young ten years—stood, dressed to the nines in pinstripe slacks and vest. The shave of his cheeks was day-old, rugged in that way that made you curious why he hadn't had time to shave. His shoulders were broad and firm, teasing the seams of his starched shirt, filling it out nicely. Near his breast pocket, the outline of a handgun creased his vest. His waist was thin, but solid, with make-me-melt cowboy-type hips.

He walked over, bent down, and kissed Velma's cheek. I stiffened, the teensiest bit offended, waiting for him to introduce himself and greet me.

"Candy," said Velma. "This is Mr. Patterson."

The H.Q.

(7)

When I was little, I didn't know enough to be jealous of Velma. I thought it was the natural order of things—she knew how to order around pilots and chauffeurs and I only had our Tuesday-morning cleaning lady, who laughed out loud when I told her to make me cookies. Velma had an air of authority and I didn't; why question it?

Since then, I have learned, not only does Velma's less-than-firm hold on her employees depend on her charming demeanor, but also that they all have their own agendas. Velma just happens to be very good at persuading these people—who are not actually *her* people; officially, they're her grandfather's, or something like that—to help her in whatever quest she has on the brain.

And this time around, Velma's quest of the week was saving my life.

"I'm Mr. Patterson," said the pumped, bashful, warm-looking guy in the suit. When he spoke, his voice had a faint, hushed accent that was impossible to pin down, but might have been Boston or British or Australian. He nodded toward that hulk of a security guy at the door. "That's Handler. Welcome to H.Q. It's cramped, but we do call it home."

I placed a hand in front of my mouth in surprise.

"*You*'re Mr. Patterson?" I felt my lips move, words come out. "But you're supposed to be *old.*"

I gasped, horrified at myself. I put my other hand over my mouth, too, to stop myself from saying anything even *more* colossally stupid.

Mr. Patterson—or the ripped, tight-muscled beach god who was impersonating Mr. Patterson—laughed inoffensively. "That's very kind of you to say," he said, laughing. His laugh was hearty, like thick soup. "Nice to finally meet you. I hope our activities in saving your life have been working out well from your end."

"Well," I swished my hair—still in recovery mode— "I'm still alive, aren't I?"

"Yes, you are." He reached a hand across his desk, offered it to me. "It's good to see that, Ms. Cohen."

I took a step back, looked at him coolly. "Yes," I said. "It's a pleasure to meet you, too."

In our room—in Velma's room, that is, done up to look exactly like the bedroom in her grandparents' house where she grew up—I tossed myself onto the bed and threw a pillow at her. My mouth was a portrait of righteous indignation.

"Why didn't you *tell* me he was hot?"

"Who? Mr. Patterson?" Velma was horrified. "I've known him since I was, like, five!"

"And he was what, six?" I burst into a fit of giggles. "My *God*. Chief of Security. I could think of at least a dozen other things to put him in charge of—" My giggles suddenly evaporated, shut up by a sudden light bulb flashing off in my head. "Oh, no, Velms—can he hear this?"

"He could if he wanted to. Although I'm sure he has far too much integrity to actually eavesdrop on our conversations."

I looked around, letting myself take note of the exquisite weirdness of this place for the first time. "Velma," I said, very slowly, "what is going on here?"

"I don't know that much more than you, Candy. Preston is insane. And I'm not an expert or anything, but it looks like he hired a bunch of people to go after you."

"I . . . *know* . . . that," I said through gritted teeth. "But where the hell are we? And who the hell is Mr. Patterson?"

Velma blanched. Her cheeks got even redder and more embarrassed. "He works with my family," she said. "This is, like, one of their bases of operations." She waited another minute, chewed on a piece of cuticle, and then her eyes bugged wide open and she squealed. "Do you really think Mr. Patterson's hot?"

"Do bears crap in the woods?"

"No, they walk out to the stream, don't they?" Velma replied. She looked honestly puzzled when she said it, cocking her head at me in stupefaction.

Oh, my Velma.

We showered and Velma left her room, dressed in a fresh set of clothes. I stepped out of the shower, tied a robe around me, and set off to explore the halls in my bare feet. The floors were padded with plush carpeting. It felt kind of like walking through somebody's living room—if somebody's living room had monitors and safes and tactical computers and looked like a nuclear monitoring station.

Everyone ate dinner together. There were no windows to the outside in the place. You couldn't tell if it was sunset or night or whatever, but they dimmed the lights and people changed into casual dress, white helmut lang jeans and a loose black pullover for Velma, a V-neck sweater and khakis for Mr. Patterson. Handler still wore a full suit. He reminded me of the Men in Black from my apartment, and I shuddered. I sat down still in my bathrobe, which Mr. Patterson had raised his eyebrow over upon my entrance. I raised one right back at him and he didn't utter a word. Dinner was spaghetti and red sauce, an uncharacteristically proletarian meal, given the nature and elegance of the rest of Velma's private army's bunker or whatever it was.

As soon as we sat down to eat, Mr. Patterson apologized to me. "Our cooking detail here is sort of manned by the same people as our security detail, I'm afraid," he said. "They're the anti-Iron Chef. You'd think the world's smartest secret agents could cook a five-course meal out of peanuts. My staff can track a mosquito a hundred miles through a tsunami, but give them any food in the world to cook and they'll make it taste like sawdust."

"They cook spaghetti practically every time I come here," Velma added dolefully, "because there's almost no way to screw up spaghetti."

Our plates were brought out by stealthy guys who looked like they should either be playing college football or guarding the president. The food was awful—yes, you really *can* screw up spaghetti—but the thing that was both scary and cool was, they did everything like secret agents. They could put your plate down and refill your water without you noticing they'd been there at all. There was a drinks cabinet, and Velma went over and fixed herself a gin and tonic and asked if I wanted anything. I snuck a brief glance at Mr. Patterson, the token adult in the room, who looked utterly unperturbed by Velma's behavior. I told her, vodka, straight.

We all sat at a war planning table because that was the closest to an actual dining room table they had. Velma and Mr. Patterson sat on one side, and I sat across the table on the other. We were a little farther apart than was really comfortable, and to talk we kind of had to strain across the table. Plus, Velma was getting all pally with Mr. Patterson, stroking his arm and stuff, and then whenever they talked about anything of importance—our next destination, for example—their voices dipped below audible level. It was just like they were adults, whispering about me like they were deciding what time to put me to bed.

I tapped my plate with my fork so that it clanged, but they ignored me and kept buzzing. After a few more minutes of cutting up hard, pasty spaghetti strands and clanging the hell out of that plate, I realized exactly what was bothering me—they both knew me way too well. Velma had lived with me forever, and Mr. Patterson, although he was a total babe, was also dapper and perceptive. My usual tricks didn't work. And I was feeling smarmy and irritable from being cooped up with Velma so long and not going to parties or meeting new people and I just wanted OUT.

I pushed my plate away and stormed out of the room.

Everyone's eyes burned into the back of my head. I didn't care. I could feel my face burning up, too.

And they weren't allowed to see that.

I stalked along the halls of the complex, feeling more out of place than ever. Somehow I ended up on the balcony above this room that looked like the War Room—glinting maps everywhere, men and women in business suits scuttling back and forth with important-looking papers. I watched the people moving below me like ants, like mindless drones serving the queen of the hive. I felt pity surge up in my chest, thinking of how they reported to work early every morning, stayed here late in the night, until their clothes were rank and smelly, toiling away on whatever project Velma's family wanted them to. Some of them probably had not been to a decent club for months.

I was kind of afraid they'd make me stay here and hide out, because "here" seemed to be so secret that not even the people who worked here knew where they worked. The secretary I talked to said she lived a half hour's drive from the base, in Philadelphia, an agent sitting with us at dinner (lunch? breakfast?) said with a perfectly straight face that he took the commuter train from downtown Juneau. There were windows, sure, but they only looked out on other windows. I sat in one of the café-like rest areas, calculating how quickly my skin would go yellow from lack of exposure to the sun, when a man came over, squeezed my shoulder, looked at my tabulations and said, "Oh, don't worry—they make sure we get enough vitamin D. I think it's something they put in the food."

I stared up at him, confused and too lonely to act offended that he'd touched my body. The man came around and sat down.

It was Mr. Patterson.

It was the first time I'd looked at him head-on since we'd been there. I'd been so preoccupied with trying not to stare. His tie was loosened, black hair frumpy, and his collar sloppily creased. Instead of looking slick and secret-agent hot, he now looked frazzled and three-day-old stubble hot.

My lip trembled. I felt like everything was rushing to the surface, and I wanted more than anything to keep it buried.

"That must explain the taste," I muttered darkly.

"No," said Mr. Patterson, "there's no excuse for that taste."

"Hmph." I sipped the glass of vodka that I'd taken from the dinner table, the one I hadn't even realized I was still carrying.

"Hey. Are you old enough to drink?" he demanded.

"Are *you*?" I asked. I downed the rest of the vodka and swished the ice cubes around the bottom of that tumbler, watching the translucent shapes swirl together and blur.

Mr. Patterson regarded me coolly. "For your information, Candy," he said, "I've been working here for six years. I really am old enough to be doing this, and I'm good at what I do. Under my command, nobody in this operation has ever died."

"Well," I said, "sorry I'm gonna break your record."

"What do you mean?"

I pushed my chair away, stood, and walked back over to the railing above the scurrying ants.

"Don't you get it, Mr. Patterson?" I asked, not even looking at him, feeling more and more awkward that I didn't even know his first name. "What they call my type of case is *terminal*. When I step out on the street, the cars ask each other, which one of us should try to run her down this time? I've had guns pulled on me more times this week than most people get in their entire lives. The last guy I went on a date with tried to kill me, and the other guy . . . I don't know. He's one of Velma's friends, and he's so weird, and all we do is talk. He probably isn't even real. And I haven't seen my father in a week and I'm messing up Velma's life and she shouldn't even have anything to *do* with this and . . . dammit. And I'm, like, *blubbering*."

I sniffled. There was snot in my nose and I could feel it running out and I didn't even care about him seeing.

"And I'm such a messy egotist that the fact that my mascara is running feels like the worst part of the whole situation."

I stuffed my head down between my cupped hands, staring down at the worker bees, trying like hell not to start sobbing.

Not even when I heard Mr. Patterson's warm and liquid voice surround me.

"Candy."

I looked up from the ants.

Hovering in front of me in the air was a handkerchief. I took it, smiled at Mr. Patterson, and blew my nose. The sound was exuberant. If the ants below hadn't been distracted with life-or-death computer programs, I'm sure they all would have stared.

I blew again and handed the handkerchief back to Mr. Patterson. He dropped it discreetly into a pocket.

"As far as guns go, yes, some weeks are worse than others. But we're going to get the average back down to zero, that much I can promise you, Candy. And as far as getting Velma involved—well, look around you."

"Yeah? It's all mindless worker drones."

"Come on, Candy. You're a smart girl. Who do you think is the queen bee?"

Velma.

The unlikeliest, wackiest person ever to be involved in life-or-death games, and as it turns out, Velma had been playing them since she was born. What did she say about Mr. Patterson? *He works for my family.* We were taken to a headquarters—a secret underground headquarters, mind you—and she had barely raised a well-plucked eyebrow. My best friend, who wouldn't even cheat on her exams, and here she was in charge of the largest purveyors of organized crime.

"Velma isn't in over her head. If she were, there would be a thousand of us following her around, backing her up in a second. We're not going to let any harm come to her, and while you're her best friend, we're going to make sure nobody lays a hand on you, either."

I wiped my eyes with my hand, cleaning out the detritus and the runny mascara. "Guess I'd better not get Velma mad at me, then, huh?"

Mr. Patterson (I *so* needed to find out his first name) wrapped his arm around my shoulders and pulled me in for a brief sideways hug. "I wouldn't worry about that," he said. "It might bring about a case of divided loyalties."

"You're so sweet." I flopped my head on his shoulder and sighed audibly.

"Now, want to see what we can do about your father? I bet I could have a secure line ready before you even start crying again."

"I was not crying," I protested.

"Yes you were. I have evidence."

"Do not."

"Do so."

"Dead bodies tell no tales," I said, hurrying to follow him down the hall.

*
* *

We slept there that night, and it was the easiest sleep I'd had in weeks. I closed my eyes, sunk into the covers, and was gone before I knew it. The dreams I had were another story—dark, vicious dreams where I woke up alone and threatened and needing to fight, and nobody would tell me where I would be attacked.

When I woke up, Velma's bed was already empty, and I slipped my robe over my pajamas and roamed the corridors looking for her. I found her already dressed, one of my brooches fastened as a barrette in her hair, standing in one of the million side rooms that lined the H.Q.

Velma stood before an exceptionally Matrix-looking case next to the door, positioned so I couldn't see what was on it. I leaned against the doorframe, smiling sleepily. She plucked off something small that gleamed, and I watched as she slid the gun into her thigh-tight jeans. It left almost no visible crease. I gasped.

"Don't look so horrified, Candy," she said. "I *know* how to use one. I took a course."

Velma giggled.

I continued looking perturbed.

"Sure you don't want one, too?" came Mr. Patterson's voice, soft and inviting, behind me.

"I don't need one," I said without turning around.

I brought up one stiff, straight hand, turned it horizontal in front of my face, and cut the air with a palm chop.

The air whistled.

Most of an hour and two showers later, Velma and I stood back in Mr. Patterson's office, ready to leave. Two small Prada beige-colored suitcases stood in the center of the floor with their handles extended. Miserably, I realized how the sum of our lives was cramped inside them.

Mr. Patterson looked even more sexily frazzled, although he had shaved. He ran a hand through his hair. A few strands at the back stood at attention. He straightened up, set a businesslike expression on his face, and rapped on the edge of his mahogany desk.

"Well, ladies," he said. "It looks like you're ready to go. Any last requests?"

A man in a business suit lifted our suitcases and carried them up to the plane. The engines revved up, and the spin of propellers roared.

I tapped my fingernail on the curve of my chin, one of those nervous things I always do before I ask a really big favor. I batted my eyes, which I always do before asking favors from guys.

"Actually, yes," I said. "Is there a way to log onto my Instant Messenger for a minute?"

"I can't believe you," said Velma when we were in the air again, twenty-five thousand feet above somewhere in Middle America. "You are the only person I know who can carry on an internet relationship and be an online stalker while in the process of being stalked yourself."

"It's not like that!" I said adamantly. "As soon as I saw Matty, he said he was waiting for me to come on. And besides, I thought he was your friend."

"Well, what did you tell him?"

"Nothing, of course. What do you think I'd tell him?"

"No—I just meant, what did you talk about?"

"Oh." I felt the outer corners of my mouth curve upward. I realized I must be smiling. "Nothing."

"Nothing?"

"I mean, we just talked."

"Right."

"Well . . . I told him I missed him."

"Mm-hmm."

We flew in silence after that, and I wondered if Velma was thinking how weird it was that her online just-friend was getting to be my online boyfriend.

Or maybe she was just puzzled how I, the kiss-and-run champion of the millennium, had managed to run smack into a web of actual infatuation.

I mean, I was certainly wondering the same thing.

Maybe I just liked the way it sounded. For once, a guy wasn't only interested in me for the way I looked. Typing to someone—it was almost like carrying on one of those eighteenth-century novel types of dating.

It was more than that, though. When I wrote to Matty, I felt like I was bigger than me. Like I was playing a character on paper, rewriting myself in a good-parts version without all the baggage.

And I liked that.

Handler flew with us to Italy—the country of love. Of course, I was headed there alone. Or, worse than alone. My traveling companions were the world's most chronically lovesick girl and a ridiculously enormous undercover secret agent who couldn't manage to look undercover as anything but a secret agent. Rome might have been where romance was invented, but I felt my own prospects for a healthy dating life fizzling out as quickly as the wine in our carafe started to breathe.

The flight attendant poured me a glass, then started pouring Handler a glass, oblivious to the gruff look on his face that said he would rather be drowned to death in that wine than drink it with a teenage girl.

"I'll pass," he grunted. "Uh. Thanks."

Velma, sitting across the aisle, swiped the glass right off the flight attendant's tray. "In that case," she said off his look, "I'll take two."

Handler hadn't wanted us to fly first class at all, it drew too much attention, but once Velma and I over-ruled him, he insisted that at least he sit next to me. "Sit by Velma, I'm fine on my own. I know kung fu, jujitsu, and krav maga," I told him.

Handler was all like, "Velma can take care of herself. Yer the one they're after."

"That's so sweet of you to say," said Velma, downing both glasses of wine, one after the other.

Actually Velma was on cloud nine. Her gun had passed the security clearance. She'd emptied it from her pockets, right along with the keys and her change, the guard waved her through, took one look in the tray—.357 magnum, chirpy teenage girl—and handed it back to her on the other side of the metal detector. She was so proud.

Roman Holiday

(8)

It wasn't until Italy that I started to seriously wonder what, exactly, our long-term plans were, or whether Velma's contacts even *had* an inkling of a long-term plan. For now, Preston was trying to kill me or scare me, I wasn't sure which. I guessed the first but Handler shook his head at me like I was a child. "They know what ya can do," he said gruffly. "They din't throw nothin' at yeh that yeh couldn't bat back."

"Nice of you to say," I observed. "When they fish my bullet-riddled body out of the Tiber River, I'll make sure they know where to send the consolation note."

"Huh. More likely, yer just gonna just charge yerself to death," he said. "'M surprised ya can handle a weapon that ain't a credit card."

"I'll slit you in *half* with my credit card."

"Yeh see?"

After landing, I followed the trail of people winding out of the terminal. The man ahead of me rounded the corner toward the baggage claim. We didn't need to do that. Velma and Handler and I carried all our bags with us. Wait—why wasn't the man ahead of me Handler, like he'd been a minute ago?

"Candy, baby," a voice drifted in my ear beside me. "You always do look so sweet."

Preston.

The scent, the musk, the creepy voice, the even creepier hair. They all stood together in one classic package of a man, walking right next to me.

My hand jammed in my purse for a credit card. If you whip the edge across skin quick enough, you really can make a deep incision. Do it in the jugular, and it could be a fast fight.

Preston's arm curved around mine, his wrist holding my forearm in place. To the rest of the world, we looked like lovebirds. I wanted to kill him.

"Don't even try," he whispered. "There's too many people. If the cops don't open fire on you when they see my corpse, one of my men will."

"Doesn't matter," I said. "You'd still be dead."

"Come on. You care about your own life too much to do that."

That wasn't true. It wasn't a lie, it was him sounding hopeful—but it wasn't true. There wasn't one thing in the world I wanted more than this all to be over. However, I did want to know what he wanted from me. Sue me, I was curious.

"So, come on, Preston. You're here for a reason, I know you have something to say to me."

"If you think I'm going to apologize, you're sorely mistaken. You had it coming."

"No, no, I'm much too mature to expect an apology from you. What do you want from me? Why are you doing this?"

Preston really looked surprised at that one. "I should have thought it was obvious."

"Think harder."

He blinked. "Date me or die."

I tensed. I felt his grimy, sweaty fingertips all over my arm. I was ready to peel him off me, whisk out my credit card, and do him in anyway. And at the same time I was almost ready to give up. I was tired of running. Date him? I'd just dump him eventually anyway. He wouldn't be the first guy I've said yes to because it was easier than saying no.

No.

No, because I was sick of seeing Velma do that exact same thing. No, because of the chance of Matty, whether he was real or a computer virus eating away at my mind. And no for me, because of all those times I gave up having fun to work a late shift at the restaurant, or the fact that all my vacations since high school have been spent on a beach with textbooks studying and blocking out my sun, and everyone deserves happiness in the times we allow it to ourselves.

My arm tensed. His hand tightened, expecting me to try to break free.

That was what I was counting on.

Preston gripped me harder, squeezing my skin protectively. My other hand shot over and held his hand in place. I yanked down in one quick lunge, pulling his arm nearly out of his socket.

He screamed.

It was loud enough to turn the heads of everybody in the terminal.

Preston fell to his knees in pain, grabbing at his own arm.

He gritted his teeth. Preston was still a tall man, even on his knees, although my Balenciaga sandals kept it from getting absolutely balanced. "You'd better watch out," he told me. "That was nearly an unprovoked attack on your part. I know better than to strike in Rome. But, if provoked, I will strike, and I will strike without mercy."

"Yeah, right, so is Rome, like, a Family hands-off zone or something?"

I meant it to tease him, but he stared at me like I was stupid. Rome. Italy. Mafia. Geez, of *course* I was stupid.

Seeing Preston on his knees and in agonizing pain made me feel better, but not much. I kicked some trash onto his pant leg, scuffed my shoe on the floor, and walked away. "Be seeing you, Preston," I said.

"The second you leave these borders, in any direction," he said—through clenched teeth, but still sounding as casual as calling good-bye—"you *will* be seeing me."

Somehow, I didn't doubt him.

"We should leave this city," I said. "We have to make him attack me."

"Vetoed," said Handler at once.

"Are you insane?" said Velma.

"This is maybe a bad time?" asked the waiter, in English, but just barely. His pen was poised to take down our order, but now it hesitated, wobbling in the air above the tablet.

We were in a fine Italian restaurant, the kind that was actually *in* Italy, you know, as opposed to the late-night hangouts around school, Tony's Italian Pizza Shack or whatever. We sat at a round table off the Tiber River, a canopy of vines draped around us, sunlight dancing on the tabletop, waiters passing by with delicately slicked-back hair. After the moratorium on going to public restaurants in San Francisco, however short it was, this felt like a clean breath of freedom.

"No, isso è non necessario," said Velma. *"Ora prendiamo il nostro alimento."*

After we ordered, Velma and I kept looking around while Handler sat there, nursing his beer and looking, in spite of being six foot five and three hundred pounds, as though he were about to cry.

At the airport Handler and Velma had found me in a matter of minutes, right before Preston screamed and I brought him to his knees. But, like everyone else, they both stood back and waited for me to finish him off.

And—as Preston picked himself up to walk away, one arm clutching the other in agony, his footsteps ringing out—every person there was dead silent. The only sound was Handler cracking his knuckles, clear and loud and painful. It echoed throughout the cavernous terminal. I knew he hated being here, and he probably hated me too, but at that moment, I could feel, he hated himself most of all. He'd failed in his duties. He'd let Preston get to me.

It wasn't even a trick. We just hadn't been paying attention.

Handler had barely said a word since.

We ate our meal in silence, unsure and antisocial, all of us behaving like people desperately in need of Prozac prescriptions. The elegant setting made it seem even more depressing. Snatches of Italian conversation swam around us, and we lost ourselves in the half-familiar words that we could almost understand if we tried. We didn't try.

And then I told them my idea.

"You know that's insane," Velma said.

"Insane enough to work?" I asked hopefully.

"I mean, why would you even *want* him to find you? Being as though we've spent all week running away from him, and all that."

"Well, how else will it end? I'm sick of feeling like baggage."

"Maybe he'll get tired of you and give it up after a while."

"Yeah, and what if he doesn't? Or what if he draws your family into it and there's, I dunno, some all-out Godfather-style gang war? Or"—my voice started to tremble, even though, more than anything, I didn't want it to—"what if *I* get tired of this first, and just quit playing?"

Velma's face fell instantly flat. I could tell she understood exactly what I was saying. "Honey, no," she began.

"I won't," I said. "Believe me—I don't want Preston to get his hands on me. Besides that he's creepy and a jerk and stuff, I just hate to lose. And I'm especially not going to lose this game. I've managed to hold off

Preston's thug squad every time I've run into them. I'm in peak physical shape, and my skills are totally at their prime. This is my Miss America moment. I'm ready."

"*If* you catch Preston alone. *If* nothing else happens to you first. I still don't think it's a good idea."

"You don't have to think. All you'll do is tell me you'll see me in a day or two, give me a big Phi Delt hug, and send me off into the war zone."

"I think that we should do it," said Handler.

For the first time that night, he sipped his beer. There was a cool silence.

"You *do*?"

That came from both of us at once.

Handler bobbed his heavy head up and down. He looked more cheerful than he had in days.

"Tactically, Miz Cohen hit the nail on the head," he said, speaking mostly to Velma. "Preston only shows up in person when he's after her. All the rest of the time, we can't touch him. He's got as big a security force around him as we do."

"Well, can't we use a duplicate Candy or something?" Velma was adamant, even after she totally realized that it was useless to argue.

"He'd know," said Handler.

I nodded. "We can wait a day or two. Enough time for Velma to get out of town, far enough away to be safe, and I can train in the meantime."

"Perfect," agreed Handler. "And we can call in enough backup."

"Uh, no," I said. "There isn't going to be any backup."

Handler opened his mouth to protest.

"I'm serious," I said.

Velma stirred her fork in the sea of greases on her plate.

I touched my mouth lightly with the white linen napkin, stood, and walked from the restaurant into the cool night street.

*

*   *

"I'm sorry!" cried Velma, scurrying out of the restaurant after me.

We both stumbled on the cobblestones. Who knows how to run in heels on cobblestones? If Italian women know how to do it, maybe they were taught in school.

Velma's cheeks were streaked with tears. I totally didn't realize, though, until after I turned around to see why she was still stomping after me. I thought she was just mad. And also I didn't understand why she couldn't just deal with me settling this with Preston. It seemed like a simple enough solution.

"What do you mean, you're sorry?" I said. "What do you have to be sorry about?"

"Well, why are you leaving me?"

"Velma," I said, trying on her kindergarten-teacher voice for size. "I'm not leaving you. There is a man who wants to kill me, and it seems like I shouldn't let you stand in the crossfire and get shot at. It's, like, common courtesy."

"God, Candy," she said. "Don't you realize, I'm already there?"

We'd barely been flying a week. And already, it felt like our lives.

"I know, honey," I told her, wringing her hands tight.

That night we went to the opera, really an excuse to get into the open. We saw *Don Giovanni*. Before that, we went for a gala dinner, the way we always used to—limousine, Valentino and Gaultier evening gowns, friskily brief dresses and enough makeup to spot us from time zones away. Before that, we scoured Piazza S. Silvestro for new toys. Clothes, cosmetics, accessories, bubble bath gels. It was almost enough to make me nostalgic for America. It was also our first actual night in public in a while—no coats, no disguises—and it should have felt victorious.

It didn't.

*

* *

During the third act, Handler was snoring loudly, Velma was playing games on her cell phone and I was eyeing every man in the audience who looked remotely like Preston with one of my hands in Tiger Paw position, ready to knock their throats into their necks if they touched me. I leaned my head on Velma's shoulder for a little while, glad we'd had our spazzy freakout. At least things with us were normal.

"Hey," I whispered without taking my eyes off the stage. "Is Handler really asleep?"

I could feel Velma's eyes being trained on me. "Why does the idea of a follow-up question make me cringe?"

I rolled my eyes up at her. "Come on, V. We are in free territory. Can we please act like eighteen-year-olds for once in our extremely short lives?"

"What? You mean, like, run away?"

My eyes glittered.

Velma tried to protest, but hers were glittering too. We grabbed our purses, stepped over Handler's sleeping form—no easy feat, considering how narrow the aisles were and how narrow he *wasn't*—and ran outside.

We stood on a brick pathway older than the country we were born in. Furry clouds wisped around the moon. The air was cool and wintry, but we fixed that quick. We stood right off Piazza S. Silvestro, and a vast matte of boutiques stood, one-of-a-kind fashions in windows, calling to us like a force of nature. We bought warm, fake fur-lined coats in the first store we found, and then wallets clicked open, hangers clicked against the metal bars of the just-arrived racks, and the strained rope handles of shopping bags multiplied along our arms. We hit all the stores along the Piazza, then slipped into a curbside café to have a glass of wine. And then we found another café for another glass, and another one. We spied on the old foreign men romancing young Italian women, and the Italian boys our age in tight shirts with hungry looks in their eyes, and we gave them death glares when they tried to approach us. We ran along the streets and sparkled brighter than the reflection of the city in the river, feeling free and unguarded and glorious, so glorious.

Handler finally caught up with us as we were making drunken wishes into the Trevi Fountain. I tossed in a handful of coins, wishing for a bunch of things that I doubted would ever come true.

On the way home Velma and I were laughing and hiccupping wine-flavored gasps of air, singing the themes to late-'80s TV shows in obnoxiously loud voices. As we stumbled down the corridors of our hotel, Velma's phone began to chirp and she answered it, "Yell-lo? Oooh, it's Mr. *Paaat*terson. I think I *knooow* someone who wants a little hankie-Pattie of her *ooo*wn . . ." and I started slapping her, hissing, "He is *not* hot!" and her saying, "That's not what you said in your *sleeeep* last night!" Poor Handler, he looked so lost that I almost wished he could get drunk and join in.

"What?" Velma was saying. She sounded puzzled. "You want to talk to Handler?" She shrugged, as though Mr. Patterson could see her shrug. "Okay, here he is."

"Yes, sir," said Handler, taking out the key and fiddling with the lock. "Sorry to hear that, sir. Yes, they're fine . . . . No, they've just been having a night out . . . . I'll turn on the television immediately. Yes, sir, I'll tell them you're patching it through."

"What's he going to patch up?" I said, and then Velma said, "Maybe you, if you're lucky," and it started us on another frenetic round of giggles.

"Candy—Velma—Candy," said Handler, waving his big mitts in the air, trying to call us to order. "Girls, sit down. Mr. Patterson wanted me to talk you down before you see this."

"See what?" I shrieked. Velma leapt up immediately to turn the television on. I collapsed onto the bed, tucking my legs together under me without even bothering to kick off my heels. "This better not be more Pay-Per-View porn . . . ."

"Sshh," said Velma.

The color was draining from her face.

The television announcer spoke in English, and the logo on the bottom of the screen was from our local Atlanta news. The newsman was one I recognized, one of those local news reporters who never goes anywhere, who's been on TV since the day you were born.

". . . other local news, police are still waiting to examine the body of Dr. Benjamin Cohen, a local physician . . ."

Oh my God.

". . . say that Dr. Cohen, sixty-two, took his own life. The family safe was found to be opened, although police have reported that nothing was stolen . . ."

In this country, surrounded by the alien language that none of us can understand, the English that now entered my ears didn't sound real. The television felt like a fabrication, like someone was tricking us.

Suddenly Velma was on the gold phone, arguing with Mr. Patterson about whether I could be allowed to fly back to Atlanta for the funeral, and I could feel, rather than hear, him saying *It's not safe, it's not safe* and I wondered what they thought about safety when here we were, having a jolly evening out in what was supposed to be the safest place in the world for me right now, and yet Preston could hurt me deeper than he ever had on the outside. I was sick of relying on guns and I was sick of relying on protectors and I was sick of people standing in my way, trying to tell me that it was okay that a man was being an inexcusable asshole and chasing me across countries and that I would be okay with enough protection. And, idly, I started to think that if they really wanted to protect me, they would have shot me right then and I would never have felt any pain again.

Without thinking, I slid open the desk drawer, took out the complimentary plastic letter-opener, and slipped to the ground, my back to Handler and Velma.

I held the opener between the second and third fingers of my left hand. The veins in my wrist and palm were pumping so fast I could barely hear them.

The blade dug into my wrist. It hurt so bad, but not as bad as I wanted it to.

I tried to breathe deeply. I couldn't breathe. I didn't know if I could do anything.

"That's it," I said.

Handler, standing by the television, wisely said nothing.

Velma snapped the phone shut. Her eyes were wide and alert. She was totally sober. She hovered over me like a concerned adult, although she knew better than to talk me out of my mission.

"Candy," she said, "do you really think you're good enough? Are you sure you can do this?"

I wanted to yell.

Instead, in one smooth movement, I tossed the letter-opener across the room. It wasn't strong, but I put strength into my throw, tensed all my muscles. Sometimes I moved my body in ways that I knew men would react to. Sometimes I moved my body in ways that I knew could kill.

The plastic letter-opener sailed right into the center of the television screen, cracking the glass in a neat, tiny bullet hole.

"Oh yeah," I said. "I'm sure."

Kidnap

(9)

The last time I really spent time with my father was right before the semester started, when the earlier sunsets were becoming noticeable and the nights were just starting to get cold. Late in the evening, I showed up at his house. The freestanding country house in the suburbs where I grew up was surrounded by vegetable and rose gardens and bushes that he neatly trimmed on Sunday afternoons, and plastic plug-in candles decorated every window.

We had the calmest evening ever. It felt so comfortable. It was a welcome change from the summer's dates and dance clubs and movie-star silliness, the calm, classical music-accented, pine-scented mellowness where I didn't have to pretend to be bitchy or sexy or restrained. I could just be Candy, his daughter, giggly and rude and utterly childish.

We sat around the TV. It didn't matter what was on, it was just background, and we swapped stories about when I was younger. I told him about my first birthday, which I really did remember.

He told me, men tried to kidnap me when I was five.

I didn't really remember that.

Actually, for a while, they succeeded. Desperate, clever men who wanted a staggering sum of money. Through his patients, my family had access to a staggering sum of money. To hear my father tell it, you'd think they were terrorists. Really, they were more like practical jokers. Waking me in the middle of the night, hiding with me in an abandoned Waffle House. There were three men and they seemed cheerful enough to me. Maybe it was just their adrenaline levels. Like I said, I don't remember much about it. Just the men—who, even then, seemed enamored of me, like, if I'd wanted to go, I could have asked—and just that feeling, the feeling of being *looked* at.

"Tell me about the rescue," I said to my father.

For this he needed another drought of brandy. He poured from a square crystal snifter, setting the glass corkscrew atop the cover of his hardback book of the week. That week was the Bible. My father sipped carefully, testing the weight of the liquid in his cheeks. The sides of his neck glowed pink with the burn. He always looked at me surprised, like he could never believe I wanted to hear the story again.

"We holed up outside the drive-thru window, about twenty of us," my father said. "The place had windows all over. The drive-thru was the only part that was obscured. We had a map of the place. We'd been studying it all night.

"I was with the police, of course," he reminded me. "They might be Atlanta's finest, but no way was I going to trust my little girl to them. Oh, they were sick of me—we couldn't get through a single step of the rescue plan without me asking questions, meeting every officer on the strike force, calculating bullet angles to be sure you would be safe and out of the line of fire. Once we had the place surrounded, they even gave me a bullet-proof vest and a helmet. I suspected it was to shut me up during the negotiations.

"The most unbelievable part is, they sent you out. As a negotiator.

"They knew they were surrounded. I don't know what kind of booze they were doped up with to think of this, but they knew straight off, you were more charming and funny and brighter than any of them. So they sent you to negotiate for your own freedom. Of course, the minute you were out, you ran to the squad car," he finished. "And do you know what was waiting there for you?"

This part I knew, not because I remembered but because it was my favorite food. It was my contribution to the telling of the story—because, even if Dad didn't charge in with his pistols blazing, he deserves some sort of reward—"Pizza sauce fries?" I suggested, nonchalantly, as though I didn't remember.

"Pizza sauce fries!" he said emphatically, as though he hadn't heard, although of course he had.

He didn't usually end the story. He left it hanging on a happy note. I sold out the kidnappers, the police were ready to bust in and arrest everyone, my dad prepared fresh pizza sauce fries for me—everyone was a hero.

But I wasn't five years old anymore. I could picture the scene that followed. The exhausted policemen, tired from the constant barrage of my father's demands, bust in on the kidnappers, who may have been assholes but were only looking to cover the mortgages on their homes. Their glares, angry, yes, but sad and betrayed, too, and I don't know why they ever trusted me. And my father: the youngest self-made millionaire in the state of Georgia, he got his medical degree at twenty and hadn't taken a vacation since. He was always the smartest, handsomest, and the most creative person in the room. Losing control as suddenly and completely as this—having your daughter wrenched from your house—could age a man before his time.

Yeah, I wasn't five years old anymore. I filled in my own endings to the story. Usually, my father didn't even need to leave anything unspoken. By the time he drank enough to start talking, he didn't have much time to talk before he quietly passed out.

That evening, I matched him, drink for drink, while he told his story. One thing I hadn't inherited: a weak stomach. Half a dozen fingers of brandy, and by two A.M., I was fine on the road, like a clear summer morning, cruising away from there to my apartment in the city faster than tomorrow. The windows of my red Mini coupe were down. The warm scratchy summer wind cut my hair in even blond threads that blew straight back in the gales, erupting like trails of smoke behind me.

Going Stag

(10)

We bought train tickets. We left that night.

We headed to the biggest city I could think of, Prague. That's where all the tourists around here went, right? He'd know where I was bound. If I had to burn a mile's worth of houses in a big flaming X, he'd know.

Fire coated my veins. I dug my nails so deep into my palm that blood leaked into my cuticles. Anger pounded in my head like a parasite that wanted to break out of my body.

On the outside, though, I was cool.

I was ice cold.

"You want a beverage?" Handler grunted.

Of course, he didn't ask until he got back from the snack car, but he was getting better at the courtesy thing, I could tell. A few more weeks in Velma's company and he'd be drinking tea out of a saucer with his little finger extended.

That is—he would, if we hadn't left Velma in Rome.

The train ride was twenty hours long. Just the two of us. For the first hour, I had to talk Handler out of calling for backup. I was still frustrated that he was there, even—I wanted to do this myself. One on one. That way, there was less chance of a mistake, more of a chance that Preston would fight me hand to hand without his mod squad. And also, so I wouldn't be responsible if anything happened to anyone.

I blinked myself fully awake, smiling at Handler. He probably thought I'd been asleep, but I hadn't. Not asleep, just away from the regular world.

God, I really hoped I wasn't going to become a total antisocial recluse by the age of twenty.

God, I hoped I would *make* it to twenty.

"At least I'll have a chance to practice my language skills," I offered hopefully.

Handler stared back at me blankly.

"I needed to pick a language, and I wanted to be weird—you know, I have all these quirks that nobody understands, not even me, really—and I thought, why not choose Czech? I might be there one day. And at least I'd be ready for the occasion."

I bent down to sort through my suitcase and pulled out my neon-plaid Heatherette topcoat with teal-colored faux fur lining.

"What was *your* major, Mr. Handler?" I asked. I patted the back of my coat down on my seat, and eased onto it. It was definitely softer than the rocky Communist seat cushions.

Handler stared back at me like he hadn't heard anything I'd said.

"So," I said to him, crossing my legs as he cracked open his Fanta, "what do you think are the odds he knows we left?"

Handler shrugged. I was only trying to make light conversation. I guess, to him, this *was* light conversation.

"What are the odds he's listening to everything we're saying?" he suggested back.

I felt the color leave my face.

He was probably very right.

*

* *

We got into Prague at sunset the next day. I mean, ex*act*ly at sunset—we walked outside and the sky was roaring with it, orange and purple streaks of cloud. The trees were bare and it was absolutely freezing. I was wearing my topcoat and knee-high leather boots, but Prague had the kind of cold that would freeze your bones to glacier temperatures.

Handler wanted to go to our hotel immediately. I said no, we should try to be seen first. To tell you the truth, I was sort of nervous that we hadn't already been approached. Without Velma, I didn't have anyone to distract me, and I was constantly on edge. Actually, no—I'd always been paranoid. Usually, I just tried to bottle it up. But roaming through the streets of a city you've never been in, mentally sorting through the items in your purse—nail file, makeup compact, gum— to determine which would be most effective as a weapon, maybe this was my destiny. Maybe I'd always been paranoid for a reason.

Okay, here was the truth, coming up like a big wave of a hangover that you can't hold down—I was worried at how good I was getting. Worried that I was starting to expect the worst instead of fearing it. Worried that I was too good at kung fu, much better than I ever was at letting people get close to me. I mean, I know this sounds crazy, but I was wondering whether God didn't create two types of people in the world—the type who were good at using their bodies for sex and the type who used them to snap other people in half.

And I was a virgin, which nobody expected, not even Velma—"You *ARE*?" she would ask, startled, and leap out of her chair or off her bed or wherever she was when we'd talk about it, and she'd look totally horrified in spite of her being the first person I'd come to if such a thing as losing my cherry ever *happened*.

These are the thoughts that go through your mind when you're left alone too long. We passed by thousands of people, beautiful high-cheekboned women, the geekiest boys, twenty-year-olds with fuzzy white-people afros pulled back into ponytails, wearing professors' tweed. Hlavní Třída Station was busy, but casually busy, flash mobs of commuters and travelers crammed together on a single set of stairs, taking their time walking up, signs pointing directions in four languages, none of them English. It was so surreal to hear people talking to each other in this language they'd spoken to each other their whole lives but most of the rest of the world had never even heard of.

I mean, who even believes that a language called Czech actually exists? It *sounds* like it was made up. Every word is a tongue-twister. I went into a supermarket, bought a pack of gum, and the clerk said something back to me that sounded like it was supposed to be *thank you* but it was about fifteen words.

I used a credit card to buy that gum.

That's the first thing I did when I got to town: started charging. Dinner. Souvenirs. Concert tickets. Groceries I'd never eat. Clothes I'd never wear. It was surprising how few places in Prague took charge cards. But when we found a place, I left my plastic hologram fingerprints all over it. If there was any better way to flash Preston, to shout at him in big block letters, I'M HERE, COME AND GET ME, I didn't know what it was.

I wasn't even thinking. I was just doing it.

This world didn't seem like a place I fit in anymore.

That was okay. I hadn't fit in anywhere for a while. Maybe ever.

Outside a trashy store called the Czech Crystal Palace in Staroměstské Náměstí, the Old Town Square, we stopped by the Orloj so Handler could reorganize all the packages. The Orloj was the biggest tourist attraction in Old Town—it was a huge medieval clock run by elaborate machinery. Every hour on the hour, bells would chime, macramé skeletons would dance, and little woodcuts of the Twelve Apostles would start to swivel and whir around the clock's intricate face. Handler was bundled from the bulging belt of his waist up to his chin with packages, because, if I was going to go shopping, I might as well do it convincingly. If there was time, we'd swing by the post office and mail this stuff back to Atlanta.

I was actually starting to believe in the hoax of a setup that we'd set up.

I pushed open the door to the Czech Crystal Palace. Handler stumbled through, rolling his eyes at me, one hand clamped on top of the ridiculously tall stack of packages and one hand holding up the fort from below. I was laughing as he passed through, laughing as I reached to the second set of doors and put my hand on them, ready to push open.

And through those glass doors I spotted a man. Just a man in a black suit, sunglasses, and bad hair greased back, the everyday uniform of CIA, spies, Wall Street businessmen, and creepy hired assassins everywhere.

His reflective lens-covered gaze met my eyes.

I flexed my fingers, rolling my shoulders back, tightening my muscles.

"Handler," I whispered.

"Yeah, Miz Cohen?"

"Drop the packages."

I heard a muffled smash behind me of glass hitting cardboard. I winced, feeling two hours' worth of deli-cately-decided-upon shopping come crashing into oblivion.

And then I saw the man's gun spit fire.

"Down!" I yelled, to no one in particular, not even moving my hand from the glass. The bullet ripped the glass, sent out a shockwave, sent a million tiny fragments of glass shuddering. It held in place, a perfect spider web of glass with a tiny void, a bull's-eye of a hole-punch that was three hundred fifty-seven thousandths of an inch thick, at its center.

Beside me, three customers—two men in their forties and a tweenage girl—had thrown themselves to the ground.

From behind, Handler said, "Kick the glass."

"What?"

"Do it with the sole of your shoe. Kick out, and then immediately pull back your leg."

I did. The glass fell in a quick waterfall straight down.

"Now what?" I said.

"Duck," came Handler's voice, loud and imminent.

I ducked, just as another bullet whistled over my head.

Then I jumped through the shattered remainder of window. The business-suit man was flanked by three other identical men, all with glasses and guns. Four, now? They were multiplying like Gremlins.

But that didn't really matter, now.

None of them were Preston.

Handler ran out shooting. His gun was small, the kind of lightweight, easily concealed pistol that all those really big guys always seem to carry in films. The gun was like half the size of his hand, and he ran in front of me, held his position and fired sparse, quick shots that seemed to land with perfect aim. Tourists streaked for cover across the square. People on the outskirts of the square dashed down alleys and side streets. Handler kept firing.

Two guys flew backwards with ludicrous speed. They were standing there, and then they weren't. Two loud cracks and they were down.

The two others rushed for me.

I somersaulted back. The packages I'd bought were lying all over. I quickly fished in the box that had flown farthest forward, the one that had been at the top of the stack, and pulled out four small crystal balls. I held two in my left hand, my good hand, and spun them around like Chinese exercise balls. I felt them getting hotter on my palm, picking up speed between my long fingers as they spun.

Causally, I made a flicking motion and sent one of them sailing. The ball flew sharply to my left, where one of the guys was charging toward me, about to tackle me. It connected right in the middle of his forehead, set him out cold. The second ball whistled into the second guy. He went down just as fast.

Which only left a dozen black-suited men, pouring toward us.

"Where are these guys COMING from?" I yelled at Handler.

He was bent over the body of one of his victims, fishing a wicked-looking semiautomatic out of two cold clammy hands.

"Can't tell!" Handler yelled back.

Tourists were arriving from all over, streaming in like ants. I checked my watch. It was ten minutes till the hour, which meant that in ten minutes, that weird clock was going to put on its mechanical little show.

Preston's men poured over the sculpture in the middle of the square, a ten-foot-tall eruption of medieval soldiers who looked like Greek gods. The sculpture was pitch black, and the oncoming night seemed to swallow it up, like a giant hole of sky in the middle of the square.

Handler stared at the gun in his hand. Taking into account the number of tourists here, it was almost useless.

One of the guys I'd knocked out was coming to. I grabbed the gun from his hands, picked up the crystal ball—which had been rolling around the cobblestones like a lazy pinball—and slammed it back into his head at close range.

His head reconnected with the stones. He looked like he would stay there.

"Candy."

Handler's face was in mine. His unibrow looked even furrier up close, and he smelled fiercely of Drakkar, a pleasing and musky, older-man-sexy sort of smell that I'd never noticed before. His forehead was creased and his eyes were sharp and demanding.

Behind his head, in the background, the men got closer.

In the corner of my eye, I saw other people coming closer, non-killing-related people. More tourists. They must have thought this was a show. Panic swept my mind.

"They're not shooting to kill," Handler whispered urgently. "They won't harm you unless they have to. That means we have an advantage. But we have to use it, Candy. Or else they'll just wake up and come after you again."

I nodded, hard. "I know. I really do know. But we have to keep everyone else safe."

"Now how do you propose—" he started.

I pushed him back and opened up my lungs louder than I ever had.

"ATTENTION TOURISTS!" I screamed. *"I SUGGEST YOU WAIT UNTIL THE NEXT HOUR TO VIEW THE ORLOJ CLOCK SHOW!"*

And then I let loose a volley of semiautomatic machine-gun fire in the air.

The tourists, scared out of their wits, ran. Even the deaf old ladies and the teenagers who only spoke French, seeing everyone else vanish fast, knew they needed to get out of there.

The men in suits—confused at how to process this sudden display of bravado that might, of all things, have only been my insanity manifesting—stood still, not sure how to react.

Handler let out a deep, bloodcurdling football yell. He charged the front line, his arms outstretched, fire in his eyes. He plowed straight into the men and he didn't stop. The men with guns didn't move, only because they didn't think that Handler would actually tackle them.

He did.

He threw them to the ground, one after another, stomped his feet into their heads and lungs and stomachs and unmentionables, and kept running.

His words still hung in my head. I saw the men off to the side, pulling out their guns, training them on Handler, delicately and deadly.

There were so many times I'd tried to avoid doing this. My father had asked me two years ago if I'd wanted to carry a gun, afraid I might be stalked (or worse) with my modeling career, and I had said no. Actually what had happened was that I said—while smiling, sweet as salt water taffy on a windy day— "But Daddy, I could always slash their necks with my credit card."

He'd laughed and tussled my hair

Oh. I was thinking about my dad again.

I spun into a drop-kick that flew me across the square. I plowed into the fray. My fists connected with faces, and my legs kicked out into stomachs. I was wearing my Versace-special-order, my most micro miniskirt of all, and I was sure that people were *totally* getting a free show, but most of those people were getting knocked out as soon as they caught a glimpse of anything.

Besides, any type of distraction was useful on my part.

I kicked low, then high, connecting with stomachs and knees and heads. My toe threw a red-hot bruise on this one guy's forehead, and I dug in with the heel of my boot, crushing his eye in a way that made me wince even as I dug in deeper. I put a serious gash in another's neck with the buckles.

I felt someone behind me. Twirling around, I landed a neat uppercut.

There was a roar from behind me. I twisted around and launched myself upward, fist first, in a neat, full surge of an uppercut to the jaw.

His head flew up and backward through the air. His body trailed after it like a kite-tail, crashing in the seasonal wooden crèche that was left over from the holiday season. I guess nobody took it down.

I took care of that.

I turned around and saw more men, flocking closer and closer to me.

Handler wrestled through a crowd of them, tossing them aside like a nest of bees he'd stumbled into. He bopped one guy on the head just as he'd gotten too close to me.

"Thanks," I said, slamming another one in the head with the sharp heel of my boot, which was turning out to be quite the weapon du jour.

"We've gotta get out of here," he gasped, catching his breath, his back to me.

"Why?" I said, kickboxing another into a wall of the Orloj clock. "They're going to stop eventually. They've got to."

"Not eventually enough," he said. Handler had given up on his machine gun, as we were all in too close range, and was swatting them off with his arms and with a stray plank of wood from the crèche. "I'll clear a space for you. Then go."

I was going to argue. But the crowd around us was only getting thicker, and none of them seemed to be friendly forces. I couldn't see where they were coming from. "You sure?"

"I'm sure." He nodded grimly.

As soon as he looked away, somebody cracked him good in the jaw. He let out a loud, earthquake-worthy bellow.

I grabbed the dude's fist in mid-punch and twisted. He shrieked.

"Ready?" said Handler.

Behind him, I nodded. I touched his back lightly, just in case he didn't see.

"GO!"

He threw up his arms, splaying men everywhere, giving me a clean alley out into the square. The far end appeared for the first time through the haze of Preston's troops.

I didn't hesitate. Bare-armed, freezing with my coat hanging half-off, I sprinted on cobblestones across the square.

I felt them reaching for me, shrugged off their grabbing hands before they even realized that I was running.

I didn't turn around until I'd almost turned the corner around the Orloj Clock.

Just then, it was chiming the hour. In the corner of my eye, I saw a man whip out a gun. Guns? I thought they wanted to take me alive.

Maybe Preston had Malcolm X'ed their previous orders: By Any Means Necessary.

It scared me at that second more than anything to know I was worth all this. A row of men, fifteen or twenty, aiming and cocking and firing guns.

There was a stone tunnel along one rim of the square that led to a side street. I dived in, somersaulted behind a pillar as a rain of bullets cascaded into the walls. They chipped the sides of the pillar, sending little pieces of shrapnel flying.

"You bastards!" I screamed. "This is pre-Revolution architecture!"

I thought I heard confusion enter into their shots, but the shots themselves didn't stop.

I leapt from one pillar to the next. They were thick, square pillars, not like those cheesy Greek round pillars which, it only occurred to me now, were absolutely horrible for hiding behind. I wonder if they even took that into consideration when they designed pillars?

Bullets dug into the pillar in front of me. A chunk of stone flew off.

I took a breath, clutched my handbag to my chest, and jumped into the alley. I pulled myself around the corner.

It was totally a different world.

Not only were the busily shopping crowds unafraid of bullets, they couldn't even hear them. Instead of cheap generic candle and crystal stores inside centuries-old buildings, I'd stumbled into Prague's equivalent of Beverly Hills Mall. Swatch, McDonalds, American Express, and Marks & Spencer signs illuminated my face across a broad plaza, filled with laughing, cajoling tourists pointing at those random things that tourists point at. On the far end of the plaza was a line of luxury hotels, their emblems glowing softly.

I looked back. They were just starting to realize that I wasn't still hiding behind the pillars.

I ducked into the crowd and made my way as inconspicuously as I could toward the hotels.

I slid through the revolving doors into the most impressive-looking one. The heated air blasted me in the face and legs as I tugged my coat back into place and shook out my hair.

I couldn't stay here long. The most expensive hotel on the street—it was way too obvious, the exact kind of place they'd expect me to choose. And it was way too empty.

The concierge was talking to a group of hotel workers in an office, his back against the door. He turned around as he heard me crash through the doors, and raised a one-minute finger to the crew. *"Cože?"* he asked, leaning out the door to see. He turned back to his audience, smirked, and said, *"Je heská plavovláská holka s velké ruzové prsy. Myslíte, že mame prázdný pokoj ten noc? Ja myslím, že možná dneska vecer bude moc dobré šteste pro mne."*

He cackled, and I huffed, who did he think he was? But he came to the counter promptly, and I smiled at him sweetly.

"Dobrou noc," I said. *"Jmenuju se Candace Cohenová, a někdy ja spim v ten hotelu. Hledám na—"*

When I started to speak, he became as reddish purple as my micromini. He coughed quickly, pulled at his collar, and his tone turned very friendly, very fast. When he thought I was looking for a place to stay, namely here, he couldn't offer me enough help.

"Oh," he said, smiling pleasantly, in the way of condescending office receptionists and evening-news anchors all over the world. "I'm sorry about that, Ms. Cohen. Will that be a suite for tonight?"

But I wasn't about to let him off the hook—or to lapse into English—so easily.

"Děkuju moc. Ale dnes, nepotřebuji pokoj. Jen jsem se procházela a přišla jsem do této ulice a pomyslela jsem si že se mi chce tancovat. Dnes večer je taková zima a takový vítr a jen jsem se chtěla zahřát a být s jinými turisty. A pomyslela jsem si že musím najít nějaký taneční klub. Ale nevím kde tu nějaká diskotéka je. Víte o nějaké? Jsem jenom mladá a krásná dívka, nemyslíte? A holky milují kluby! Já vím že já miluji kluby. Ale neznám žádné dobré kluby v tomto městě. Takže jaké kluby znáte? And is there one around here? Je tu nějaký v blízkosti? Musím najít nějaký dobrý český klub, kde nejsou žádní turisti a cizinci, děkuju."

I told him that I needed to find a place to hide. And I asked for the first thing I could think of, a totally unassuming place where I would blend in seamlessly, to the first thing that any decent, respectable, well-dressed American girl my age would do in Prague—to check out guys at a dance club.

"Je klub s moc velky muzy, jestli chces, 250 kilometry na prave strane, na Kostecna. Jmenuje se Základní Klub."

"The Základní Club," I said, tasting the name in my mouth. The Základní Club was a club near here. I was going to hide in the Základní Club.

"Ja, to je," he said, nodding. *"Dobré steste, pana Cohenová."*

"Ciao," I said, already strutting out the frosted glass doors.

The world outside was still the familiar blizzard of people. I looked left, looked right. I saw a red and white street sign that said *Kostecna*, small and plain, off the corner of the broad boulevard. A few buildings in, I heard loud English, coming from around the corner. It sounded loud and it sounded angry, and I knew it was Preston's men. I bit my lip, wondering what I could do, if I could do anything.

And there it was, shining like a secret nightlight.

A small pink sign with block letters in Communist black: *Základní Klub*.

I put one hand on the doorframe. My nails by now were shredded, barely longer than my fingers. I hoped this place wouldn't be the kind of place where something like ragged nails made a girl stand out too badly.

With my other hand, I pushed the door open.

This didn't feel at all like a tourist bar. Men bristled and brushed against each other brusquely, As far as low-key and local went, the concierge had hit the nail right on the head. Some of the men were balding and hairy, wearing leather vests. Others were dressed in tight-fitting polo shirts, looking clean-cut and handsome, not a stray strand of facial hair on them.

Knots tightened in my stomach. Straight men did not know how to shave this well.

I realized, this was the kind of bar where *being* a girl made you stick out.

Základní was the Czech word for *crazy*, and I had a feeling that things were about to get *základní* pretty soon. I had brought my cycle of violence and mayhem to one of the only gay bars in the Czech Republic.

Oh, well, I thought. *Maybe they'd never think to check inside here.*

"Good evening," the bartender spoke to me in a thick Czech accent, rubbing down the bar with a dishrag. "What do you like for drink?"

The door slammed open with a violent shudder.

We all turned around.

Two men came through the door, lugging something big behind them. Another man, the one who'd thrown open the door, stood aside as the others cast the bundle to the floor.

It was Handler.

And he was dead.

When the first man spoke, it was in a quiet, even voice.

"Candy," he said. "Look what you made us do."

Nervously, I took one step deeper into the crowd. The men beside me shuffled, not wanting to step away from me, but not wanting to get a bullet right between their eyes like Handler had.

The men poured into the room. The first three, then another three, then two, and then two more. That was their entire number, after the few that Handler and I had cut down. Ten men. They had already killed Handler, and they were coming for me.

"Oh, no," I heard a voice—a voice in English—which I thought, for a very split second, was my own. "This just won't do."

I realized after a second, it wasn't.

For one thing, it was a man's voice.

Two quick wallops of gunshots cracked quickly. The first hit man, still holding the door open, crumpled at once.

The others drew their guns.

I stepped out from the crowd, already in my attack position. One of my fists hovered in the air opposite my chest, the other one tucked just beneath. I flexed my muscles, feeling them breathe.

Then I saw a man in a three-piece suit slide down the bar.

He slid neatly to the edge like he had ice skates on his ass, and jumped to the floor in one fluid movement. His hair was impeccably in place, his fists raised, his tie held docile by a tie tack, not even fluttering.

"Mr. Patterson?" I gasped, afraid to move.

"Pleasure to see you again, Candy," he replied, not turning around.

Two sturdy kicks disarmed the two men in front. Their guns skidded out to the edge of the walls. Immediately, a quick-thinking bear and a like-minded raver boy snatched them up. The bar-goers weren't going to fire them—I mean, they didn't even rightly know who the good guys *were*—but at least there were two guns out of commission.

The rest of the crowd had packed themselves even tighter than before, surrendering pint glasses to the tables and the bar. They had condensed into a far corner of the room, nervously watching us fight.

"Easy, Candy," Mr. Patterson said. He was in full-on hand-to-hand combat with two more of the men. He lectured me with a tone of voice that was half Zen and half nanny. "Just take it easy, don't let them rush you. They're not going to kill you."

"That's what Handler said!" I cried, nearly screaming.

I punched one guy's face so fast and hard it was a red stump before he collapsed. Then I fired a series of kicks at another one's face. One Dolce and Gabbana heel later, he was lying in a pile of stale beer, a gash as big as a fist across his face.

I was on full automatic now, like a monster, totally in uniform. In my mind's eye, I could see Handler, the frenzy overtaking him as he went down. Patterson had his tie off and was whisking it around one man's neck and choking him with it. He threw the man behind him, ducked down, and toppled the man over his head and brought him crashing down on another.

One of the men stood in a corner, fishing beneath his sport coat. "Gun!" I yelped, pointing at him for Mr. Patterson's benefit.

He glanced quickly, noting it before he stuck a beer glass onto one thug's mouth and nose and twisted, holding it there in a vacuum until he lost consciousness.

"Forget them!" said Mr. Patterson. "They're not even firing! They're meant to capture you!"

Capture me.

The thought shot through my mind like a mantra giving me something to hold onto. Their instructions were to capture me, to hold me.

That meant Preston was here, close by.

I forgot everything else.

I lay into the rest of them as they swarmed me, kicking, punching, scratching, and biting. I wasn't trying to kill them, and I don't even know if my punches alone were enough to kill a man that big. I wiped three of them out in a snap, and Patterson finished with the man in his corner. That meant there was one left.

And he was coming up right in front of me, fists ready.

It was too close to dodge and too quick to duck. In my kung-fu face-offs in school, I'd always gotten taken by surprise. I'd lost bouts based on strength and based on skill and based on not feeling like fighting and because, with a kind of morbid, crash-victim fascination, I'd been watching my mother as she sat in the audience, snapping pictures of me in my pressed white *gi*.

Those knuckles as big as mountains, millimeters from my face, with nothing in their way. I had never in my life felt so singly powerless to avoid something.

I wondered if he would break my nose.

I wondered if faces were malleable, rechargeable, and I wondered, if my face twisted out of shape, would it grow back normally or would it heal oddly, in that crunched-up paper way, the way that old people's faces wrinkled. Was his thumbprint going to stay with me for the rest of my life? I wondered if I even *had* a rest of my life to negotiate with.

I cringed, thinking how death might be literally seconds away.

I had served my last blue-plate special.

I had gotten my last summer tan.

I had aced my last test.

I had kissed my last boy.

And then his fist connected.

My face twisted. Blood splattered against the concrete wall.

That was it.

I railed into him. I forgot my fist positions and leg alignments and stances and all that. I plunged one fist into his stomach. Then I plunged my other fist into his stomach. I pulled them out and sunk them back in. I punched fast. I punched with the speed of my lungs breathing. Punching his stomach felt like a balloon when you squeezed the air out of it. It got smaller and more squishy and soft. His hands stopped grabbing for me and crumpled to his sides and then his arms fell completely. Eventually he fell into the wall and I kept punching him until I felt Mr. Patterson's soft hand touch my back.

"I think you got him, Candy," he whispered.

Outside, we walked through the winter streets, Mr. Patterson's thin, strong arm around my shoulders. Although it sounded gristly, the bartender had fished an extra pair of workman's pants from the back room, and I wore them with my Heatherette topcoat, which also seemed way too insignificant to combat the Czech winds.

But Mr. Patterson's arm, that was keeping me warm.

"I'm sure Reign got out of here the second he heard it turn bad," he said. I nestled my head onto his shoulder, trying not to think about exactly when it turned bad. "I'm really sorry, Candy. I thought we would have prepared for everything."

"You couldn't have," I said. "It's not your fault, anyway."

I blinked, staring vacantly at the National Theater in the distance.

"Candy." He pulled me to a stop, staring reproachfully down at me.

"Yes?" I avoided his eyes.

"You're not thinking that this is your fault, are you?"

"Let's keep walking."

"Candy, come on. I'm a people person. Talk to me."

"I'm *not* a people person," I said, starting to walk again. "I don't talk well."

He reached out his arm and touched my neck right at the nape. I felt my body stiffen, unable to move.

Softly, slowly, he removed his hand, slipping it back down to my back, and he began to rub. He turned me around to face him, and he looked me directly in the eyes.

"Candy," he said. "I've never lost anyone before tonight. That was the signature of my career. That was why Velma's family put me in charge. Ever since my first heist, I have made absolutely sure that everyone under my command stayed safe, healthy, and, well . . . and alive."

Mr. Patterson stopped in the middle of his sentence, as though he were remembering a long-forgotten thought.

"So, what now?" I asked. "Are you afraid of what they're going to do to you?'

"No," he said. "I'm afraid of what I'm going to do to myself."

"But—"

I stopped myself. I had absolutely no aptitude for consoling people. I was awful at making people feel better. The only helpful thing I could ever do was bring them to the mall for shopping therapy.

Especially when I felt at least that miserable myself.

And, God, everything that happened was all about *me*. If I hadn't decided to bait Preston into tracking me down. If I hadn't pulled Velma into running with me. Even at the restaurant, before all of this started, if I'd only managed to contain my acerbic self and smile and toss my hair and act like a normal vapid girl on a normal vapid date, and kissed Preston at the end of the night, then he would have gotten bored with me eventually, or bored with trying to seduce me, and he'd wind up with another bulimic teen star two weeks later.

Just about the only correct thing I'd done on this whole mission was managing to stay alive, and I'd managed to kill all these other people just to do that. Even Handler, and *his* life was practically guaranteed.

"You're feeling sorry for yourself, aren't you," said Mr. Patterson, reading my mind as usual.

"No," I protested.

"Maybe," I sighed, my face softening.

He put a finger under my chin. "Now, don't show it," he said. "You're supposed to be thick as iron, aren't you? And besides, worry causes wrinkle lines."

I felt my face involuntarily snap into an expression of alarm.

Mr. Patterson laughed, pulling me back into a walk. "Listen," he said. "The first thing that happens when you get back to civilization, we're going to do this up good. Guards around you 24/7. Full-on GPS searches for anyone who has anything to do with Preston Reign. Tracking your movements, and the movements of anyone who tries to find you. It started out something ludicrous, but we're going to make this thing airtight, and then we're going to pop it like a bubble."

As he spoke, my face fell into even deeper despair. Tracking my movements? Twenty-four hour guards? Controlling who sees me?

"That's why you're not going back," he finished.

I opened my mouth, ready to protest, when I realized what he'd just said.

"What?" I spat out.

"I'll tell you what," he said as we resumed walking, again. "First, we are going to sit through a perfectly ordinary, perfectly mindless puppet show. So that you can say you did something in Prague that did not involve having guns fired at you. Then, I will provide you with your own gold phone and untraceable credit card, and you will go off. On your own. Into the wilds. We'll have people on you, and we'll have them nonstop, but I give you my word, you will not see, hear, smell, or otherwise sense them. You've been through more tonight than any girl your age should have to go through. And it's my opinion—my professional opinion—that you need a vacation."

"Is it, now?" I couldn't help smiling, although I was about to protest when he started talking about me being a "girl my age."

"It is."

"Well, good."

"And, for your information, I happen to think that you're exceedingly mature."

"For a girl my age?"

"For a girl of any age."

We started to walk toward the National Theater, the lights getting brighter every step. I took his arm and hooked it around mine, sliding my hand back into the pocket of my topcoat.

"Mr. Patterson?"

"Hmm?"

"Tell me this, also. For my information. Why were you in a gay bar?"

Mr. Patterson smiled. "I'm sorry, darling. Even if you were old enough . . ."

"*Mature*, you mean."

"Even if you were mature enough, Candy, I'm afraid you're not my type."

"Too violent?" I asked, still hopeful.

He stopped once more, leaned down, and kissed me gently on the forehead.

"Too female," he said.

Monks

(11)

I am everything and everything is around me.

There is a field. In the field are twelve silver rabbits. They hop in unison. Their paws barely brush the grass beneath them, and each of the billion blades tenses with the weight of each tiny bunny footprint landing.

I am all of those twelve rabbits, and I am the field, too.

In my mind's eye, I see a perfectly symmetrical hut of leaves and bamboo thatch rising up behind me. The rain that falls from the clouds. Ten thousand stalks of grass and flowers and the roots of trees nestled in soil, catching the rain, drinking it up. The Cycle of Life. I hold that bunny, feeling its little heart beating, its life force close to my own, clasp it close to my formless, flowing clothing.

What the hell am I wearing?

My eyes popped open.

I was sitting with legs folded up Indian-style, my fingers curled into little yoga O-shapes. I was hundreds of miles from a shower, light years from any mall. I was wearing a featureless white robe that looked like Martha Stewart carjacking Hugh Heffner's wardrobe, zero percent spandex and a negative fifty for style.

For a second, still woozy, I recoiled in horror.

Then it hit me at once, and I thought, *No, Candy. This is totally where you're supposed to be.*

I was in the Tall Peaks Wat Phourat. On top of a mountain two hundred miles outside of the closest city, on a politically incendiary border somewhere between China and Cambodia. The sky was close, the clouds looked like fading dreams of dragons, and the air was so thin it felt like I couldn't inflate my lungs completely.

Supposedly, if you were being suffocated, right before you died, the most unearthly calm would set over you. You'd feel dead before you actually died, because your breathing would stop and your body would give out before your brain was finished with it.

I'd been thinking about death a lot these days.

Okay, that's actually a lie. I hadn't been thinking much at all lately. I think all the credit we give to these monks, those weird little bald men you see gliding around the streets downtown in their little orange and yellow robes, I think it's all a sham. They wake up *way* too early to be coherent, and they spend, like, the entire day doing this menial labor stuff. My first day here, I showed up, all ready for spiritual enlightenment and removing the yoke of this world, and what did they make me do? They gave me rice stalks and they made me peel the rice off. Grain by grain. A single sheath could take hours.

Then I looked around the room and everyone else was doing the exact same thing, all the monks, right up to the head abbot, the chief of the whole monastery, who was sitting on his own pillow with his own little rice stalk and his own little bowl. And he was shucking away, same as every other monk, same as me.

We did this for hours.

It's not like he was teaching some great spiritual lesson as we shucked. It was actually not like much of anything at all. Most horrible of all, it wasn't even *boring*—it was just endless. There were all sorts of things to think about. The angle that the rice flew off the stalks, the capacity of the bowl, and how did rice even *grow*, it was small and white and hard, it wasn't soft like an apple, there was no room for absorbing nutrients or changing colors . . . .

And before you knew it, it was midday.

Monks don't eat after midday. It didn't matter if we were hungry or not, that was the only time that we ate, and at that time, everybody ate. It cleansed our bodies and it made food a regular thing, like sleeping or walking or even shucking corn.

Early in the first week, I started to feel clearer. Not only because all the snot and aching and stuff from the sudden Czech winter was fading out of me. It was still cold outside, and the snow fell continually around the monastery. We didn't do much about it, either. We were still in these loose and ridiculous-looking—and yet oddly comfortable—robes. And we walked around barefoot. I think I actually have developed calluses. And the *robes* (Martha Stewart, Martha Stewart). But after a while, it didn't even bother me.

Toward the end of that first week, I started to feel invisible eyes on the back of my neck, people watching me. I'm not sure if was ESP or just the new diet doing *základní* things to my head, but I could sense things that I'd never sensed before.

The funny thing was, it didn't bother me. That people were watching. By now, it felt like when I walked down the street in a short skirt and somebody stared. Or like when I beat a man in a fight and people stared.

My eyes shot up. Suddenly there was some dude standing there, hovering over me, and I was ready with the sharp end of the rake I was holding facing up, ready to separate his face into four equal strips of skin. But, no, he was only reading.

I shook my head, trying to shake all those deviant thoughts out of it. I only succeeded in weirding myself out further and alerting myself to the new and conspicuous absence of long hair wisping around my shoulders. When I turned my head right, the stillborn ends of my hair—trailing right around the top of my neck—gave me a rough tickle.

Everything was getting lighter.

It was like I was supposed to be on that mountain, in that moment. I wasn't sure why, but it had felt right. I had taken a taxi from Prague to Bratislava. At the station when I told the dispatcher I wanted a six-hour taxi ride, his eyes narrowed and he asked how I planned to pay. I handed over the untraceable card and told him to him to swipe it, and once he did, his eyes bulged out of his sockets at the limit. I knew how he felt.

Mine did, too.

From Bratislava I caught a train. I took a pile of clothes out of my backpack and rolled them into a makeshift pillow, but even the combined mass of twenty Sonia Rykiel silk dresses wasn't enough to dull the ache of the rickety hardwood train bench.

After about two days of sitting on the train, riding through mountain ranges, dreaming of throbbing hip-hop clubs and having nightmares of bad men killing my friends, and reading bad Czech translations of bad English romance novels ("He pull her glistening womanhood toward him with hairy manly hands"), I'd had enough. Every bump we felt, I thought that Preston's men were about to hijack the train.

And so, somewhere between the end of Turkey and the beginning of somewhere else, I stepped off the train while it was still in motion.

There was snow on the ground. I tried my best to ignore it. I trudged through it, hiking uphill for days, not knowing where I was going but figuring that, sooner or later, I'd have to run into something.

I did.

Halfway up the mountain, the snow cleared and it began to get all nice and spring-timey. I stared at the ground as I climbed, totally fascinated by how incredibly green the grass looked, and almost bumped into this guy. He was about a thousand years old, and he was wrapped in a robe, and he was staring at me. I asked him what his name was.

He told me, "Daido."

Behind him was a big wooden building with a ceiling that tilted up at the ends and walls made of rice paper. There were a bunch of guys in the distance who were just starting to notice me. I asked him if that was where he lived. He nodded. Then I asked if I could see it.

He nodded somewhere in the distance and said, "Women there."

I got on my tiptoes and peeked behind him and said, "Yeah, well, what kinda fun stuff are you hiding from the girls?" I pressed my body past the growing crowd of monks who were standing there, watching us, and I walked straight into the monastery to check it out.

Ten minutes later, I was shucking rice.

The nuns lived on the next mountain over. On harvest days, everyone came together in the village below, along with the people who brought donations of fruit and rice to the monastery. They said that the village and the monastery had a symbiotic relationship, that we prayed for them and they sustained us. I was like, "Then why do we have to de-grain these wheat stalks?" The monks all laughed, and it felt like the kind of joke where the punch line is in another language.

So I laughed, too, because I was trying to fit in with them.

I was trying to lose myself.

Some nights I crept out after hours, pulled out the one small suitcase that I still had, bruised and battered from all the flights and fights. I unzipped the outermost pocket and pulled out my cell phone, the golden one that Mr. Patterson left me, with its battery that still comes up full and the signal bars that never fade. I was sure they knew where I was, but I had Mr. Patterson's word that they wouldn't come and get me. The last thing I told him, right before I started walking, was that I wanted to be lost.

Really lost.

The kind of lost that never got found.

I stared over at the nuns' mountain across the stream, and some nights I could see a cloud of smoke trailing into the sky. It grew up in a narrow column, reaching straight into the sky until it mingled and faded into the dark gray clouds. I thought about why the nuns were burning fire this late, while the monks were all asleep. I wondered if they were throwing a party.

I still don't know why I was with the monks, except that the abbot was there, and the abbot, the other monks told me, had specially requested to observe me. It made me feel a little bit awkward, a little self-conscious, but I tried to ignore it and keep at my normal routine of working, sleeping, shucking—just like I imagined my father doing in the hospital, those nights when he overworked himself and didn't remember to come home until after midnight.

But I didn't have time to let myself think about that. I wasn't thinking about my father, and—when I did—I had the weirdest uncanny feeling that he was in the dirt we tilled, that parts of his bones broke down and turned into soil and the wind blew it across oceans and, some-how, it ended up here, mixing with seeds and fertilizer, growing into rice.

I shucked more rice. Every time my mind wandered, I forgot what I was doing and I squeezed the stalk too hard and rice flew in the air, in between the cracks of the floor, and into the monks' poor unexpecting eyes.

The monks glared at me, pretending to not be angry, but their eyes were so red that they couldn't help looking that way.

I gulped loudly, grabbed at another rice stalk, hid my face behind it as much as I could, and started shucking again. I stared at the ground. From beneath the narrow floorboards, the rice stared back at me.

I wondered how long it took to get good at this. Had they been practicing for months? Years?

The other guys at the monastery were not big talkers. The abbot never talked to anyone. I kind of liked it that way. It wasn't antisocial at all; I can't even explain why. Talking felt kind of superfluous. Like we already understood what each other would be talking about. And it let us concentrate more on the important things at the monastery, like, you know, planting seeds and shucking rice.

In a way, it was the first time I'd ever gotten my hands dirty.

And in a way, it was the first time I'd really needed to.

Then one afternoon, I was going about my normal chores, laying out blankets and pillows after the group laundry, and the abbot—sitting in a corner, stuffing bits of fish for the night's dinner—beckoned me over.

"Candace Bettina," he said in a whisper loud enough to hear across the building. "Shall we talk?"

I bowed, as was the custom, and he looked away, as was also the custom. One of the monks told me that regular people always bow when they talk to monks, acknowledging the presence of God—or Buddha or whatever—that hangs out when you're living the monastic lifestyle. Meanwhile, monks were always careful to look away, just to make sure they weren't thinking they were taking any credit for the bowing or anything.

"Sure," I said uncertainly. "If you want."

He waved his hand toward a pillow. I curled up in it, tucking my legs underneath me. I smiled genteelly at him, just to let him know I was listening. He didn't return it. He didn't even really look at me. His eyes flickered so vacantly, it kind of felt like he wasn't looking at anything, although his presence was totally the opposite—you'd think he saw everything.

"Candy," he said again.

"Abbot," I replied. I lowered my eyes in deference.

"Are you cold?"

"N-no," I replied, thrown off guard by the question. Waking up for the first time on the mountain was possibly the coldest I'd been in my whole entire life. But since then, it hadn't been anything, like an early fall breeze that threw me off for just a second.

"It's good to hear. A few years ago, many white people showed up here. They see the Dalai Lama on television, read a book, think they know our whole story. Hnh!" he snorted, smiling as if to counter it. "Not that I am offended. Anyone gets interested in us at all, and I am flattered. Why should somebody ten thousand miles away think about me? It is puzzling."

"I know exactly what you mean. It's like when guys come up to me on the street and start talking to me like they know me because they saw me in a magazine, they think they've met me and we're, like, best friends or something, and I'm like, when you met me, I wasn't even *there*."

If the abbot was thrown by my explosion of the secular American world, he didn't show it. He reminded me of Velma's grandfather, patient and restrained, but a tigerlike intensity in his eyes. Maybe he was Family in another life.

Instead, he got up, walked over to the window, and stared out. A fresh round of snow had fallen last night, and the garden was dusted by a thin, almost translucent cover of snow. The bushes and vegetables and the green and tiny twisting vines were all accessorized in white, and nobody had been outside at all yet. The snow was crisp, free of footprints.

"We are taught that snow itself is not cold," said the abbot. "When one cups snow in one's hand, it melts almost at once. Snow, clearly, is no match for the human body, which burns at a much higher temperature. Why, then, are we turned so cold by snow?"

I walked six steps behind him, following in his footsteps, walking slowly, leaning on my toes.

"Because it looks cold?" I offered.

Then I froze, not sure if I was supposed to answer. It kind of sounded rhetorical.

"Yes, Candace," he said. "Exactly that."

The abbot looked back at me, chuckled, and turned back to the snow.

"It's all in our heads," he said. "Well, not everything. But more than we are normally willing to admit. One must wonder, without sight to make him cold, does a blind man feel warmer when surrounded by snow? Or when he feels a warm spring breeze, does he read it as a sign of an impending snowfall?"

I frowned. He was veering way too existential for me. "Listen," I said, "I'm a bio major. I'm premed. I know about blindness and stuff, but spring breezes? Poetry usually goes way over my head."

He frowned, apparently troubled by this. I worried that I'd offended him. But he seemed to reconsider.

"Candace," he said, speaking the words slowly, "do you put on different lip gloss when you're going to meet your father and when you're going on a date?"

"Of course," I said immediately. "There are some lip glosses that you wear to the clubs that just aren't appropriate for G-rated daytime audiences."

"But the lip gloss itself does not change."

"Well, no. It's always lip gloss."

"Why, then?"

I squelched my eyes, trying to hit it. "It just . . . re-contextualizes me."

"Exactly, Candy. The world is an illusion."

"Well, duh. Everything is an illusion. But illusions can still mess with your head. Sometimes, illusions can *hurt*."

"Sometimes, we let it hurt. We need to live in the illusion, or else we do not fully commit to our lives."

"Are you talking about my social life, or about my father dying?"

The abbot's expression, without actually changing, *changed*. Like I knew what he meant, but I didn't quite understand him, all at the same time.

"What makes you think I am talking about either one?"

"I dunno."

"The veils of reality are just that, Candy. When the Buddha sat under a tree for three nights and days, he realized that everything in his life was nothing more than a façade, as it were. Although there was a tree in front of him, it was like there was nothing, for the tree had not always been there, and one day, he knew, the tree would be chopped down, or it would decay, or an earthquake would swallow it into the ground. So, too, are we. We are pinnacles of nonexistence, with the faintest trace of existence in the median margins.

"Before this," said the abbot, "I was a baker. When I am done here, I could go back to baking again. One thing the Buddha teaches us, it is that nothing is absolute, and we cannot stop change. Tell me—how long do you think Daido has been here?"

Daido was one of the oldest monks there. Daido seemed to know everything about the monastery, all the customs and traditions, but all the secret hiding places and the mealtime dishwashing rituals, too.

"Fifty years?"

"Six weeks," he said. "He came just before you did."

"But how come he *knows* everything so well?"

"This world is a veil of illusion." The abbot waved his hand in the air, touching nothing. "Some people are more fluid and can adapt quickly to any situation. Others are more stubborn, and force situations to heel to their own will. Tell me, what do you think about your friends?"

"My friends?"

"The girl who you left in Rome, Velma. And this boy, Matty. They are part of your journey, but they, too, are like illusions."

"But you just said *everything* was illusions."

It was like I'd just hit it.

But I could feel myself getting impatient with the abbot. Like, if he was trying to teach me a lesson, why didn't he just go ahead and teach it?

I stood up angrily. My heels slapped the pillow I'd been sitting on, and it sailed angrily across the empty room. I opened my mouth to apologize, and then I shut it, feeling all my red emotions sailing to the surface.

"Forget this!" I shouted. "Everything you're saying makes sense, but that's because you're not actually *saying* anything. I mean, I totally appreciate the working-with-your-hands stuff and the only-eating-rice hippie stuff and, whatever, I even deal with these clothes. But stop trying to play with my mind. Stop trying to pretend everything's okay and we're all at one with the universe, because sometimes, that shit just does not fly. Right now I am pretty pissed off at the universe."

I turned at him, my face blood red, my blood burning livid.

"And you know what?" I hissed. "The universe deserves it."

By now I was storming out the door, throwing my hands in the air. In one corner, the rest of the monks— my only friends since I'd gotten here, albeit friends who barely talked to me and were all ten to forty years older than I was—ducked their heads.

I walked to the main doors of the monastery building, pushed them open with both my hands, and walked into the snow, the soles of my feet melting footprints into the fresh cover.

"Wh-what the h-h-hell are you d-doing?" shivered a voice.

A cold voice.

A *girl's* voice.

The hooded, goggled, snow-suited figure pushed the furry hood of its parka back. Underneath was just about the reddest face I'd ever seen in my life.

"Velma?" I said.

Field Trip

(12)

I stared at Velma like she was a ghost. My brain was processing things slower and slower, and I wondered if it wasn't just a side effect of the rice-and-more-rice diet.

"What the hell are you *doing* here?" I demanded. "Mr. Patterson told me he wouldn't disclose my location to anyone. He *promised* me!"

"I kn-kn-*know*," Velma huffed, her teeth chattering. "Nobody would. According to Mr. Patterson and every other operative in my family's employment, you disappeared off the face of the earth. Do you realize how hard that is to *do*, Candy? Patterson must really like you."

"Yeah," I said quietly. "We, kinda. We went through some stuff together."

"God, Candy," Velma said. "What has happened to you?"

Facing her, the wind upducing the fresh snow, rustling my new short hair, I realized just how much had happened since I'd seen her.

I realized that I'd run out on her exactly at the moment my father died.

"Velma," I said. "I killed Handler. We were fighting these guys and he couldn't go on and then I used up all my Christmas presents beating them up and then I ran and I hid in a gay bar and Mr. Patterson was there and we were in a shootout and I found this monastery and I started becoming holistic and I can breathe through my brain and stuff and I don't even think I get cold anymore, and they've been teaching me how to use the other half of my head and modeling is like seeing through the veils of reality, and I don't even know if I can still act flaky when I need to."

Velma stared at me, open-mouthed, until I had absolutely finished talking.

"Why was Mr. Patterson in a gay bar?"

"Because he *is*, Velma."

"What? Just like that quarterback you dated sophomore year??"

"Mm-hmm, I suppose so."

"Candy, what do you *do* to boys?"

"I swear! I just ran in, and there he was, macking on Eastern Europe's finest."

"Wait. You're really serious, he's gay?"

The crushed look on my face told her everything.

At that moment, I could feel both of our hearts breaking.

Then Velma started to giggle, and then I started giggling too, and before you knew it, there we were, two giggling white girls in the neck-high rice fields, getting swept up by snowdrifts.

And then, just as suddenly, I stopped laughing.

I looked at Velma, her face at the level of my shoulders, her hair just a little bit different than I remembered it. "Velma," I said, "my daddy's dead," and for the first time, with Velma's familiar oldness in my head, it felt real, realer than spirit and afternoon fasting and communicating with the Divine Reality, that somewhere in Atlanta, there was a house with my father's bed that he was never going to sleep in again.

I began to cry.

I wasn't crying for me. I was crying because my father was gone and would never be anywhere ever again, and because I was an orphan now, and that meant that there were two people, the two people on earth who I was supposed to understand and love more clearly than anything, and neither one was here anymore.

I heard a deafening motorized sound, like electric toys, only on a huge scale. I looked up from Velma's shoulder, and plowing through the snow was a little bald monk in a Land Rover snow buggy, three-foot high tracks treading through the snow. He pulled up right beside us and sat there, grinning stupidly.

"Soupha, what are you doing?" I said.

"The abbot, he say you learn well," said Soupha. "Now you ready to go home."

"You are?" came Velma's voice behind me.

"I—I am?" I stammered.

"Climb in," Soupha told us.

"But it's a three-day trek each way down the mountain!"

"Night and a half, on here," Soupha replied. "Climb in!"

I hesitated. Velma, though, needed no second word of encouragement. One tiny leg after the other, she leaped up onto the treadmill, then into the rear seat, throwing off her metal-framed backpack.

My bag, I saw, was already loaded.

We started the treacherous downward climb. Trees blew by in a frenzy. The Land Rover dove right through the snow, shucking it aside like strands of rice from a stalk. My mind burned furiously, thinking of the abbot's admonition. Had I really learned well? I didn't feel like I'd learned at all. I still felt unnaturally torn out of this world, the world I was about to dive back into. Yet, at the same time, I didn't want to be a part of it anymore.

I was sick of running. I was sick of everything.

"So," Velma said when we finally stopped for a break, "I'm thinking, we reach the village at the bottom of the hill, and we should contact Mr. Patterson as soon as we can."

"No!" I cried, a bit too aggressively, because both Velma and Soupha looked at me with concern. "I mean, we don't want to broadcast our location yet. If we just stay cool and, you know, lie low, we might be able to score more time before they're onto us."

"Before *who's* onto us?" Velma said. "The people who are trying to kill you, or the people who are trying to save you?"

I held my breath, then let it all out in one big *whoosh*.

Then I let the news drop.

"I think they might be two sides of the same coin," I said.

"What?"

"Look. I don't think Mr. Patterson and Handler and all your friendly Family people are working with Preston. But you said yourself, they're like two branches of the same family. So what if Preston's people are watching your people to see when they react?"

Velma's face turned even paler than the snow. "You are *so* not from this planet."

I nodded. "I know. But it all seems to work out."

"Okay." Velma moved to the edge of her seat, and I could tell she was switching into planning mode now. "So what should our first step be?"

"From here, I don't know," I said. "Getting to the airport shouldn't be hard. And if you think those untraceable credit cards are really untraceable—"

One quick shake of her head said *yes*. "They wipe out everything immediately," she said. "Mr. Patterson himself couldn't track them. Hell, they even program the registers to print the receipt in vanishing ink."

"And the gold phone?"

"Untraceable too," Velma said. "It has a special button to communicate with Mr. Patterson's people. All we have to do is not push it."

I wrung my hands grimly. "Okay," I told her. "So, we agreed, we're cutting off the Family. But we need someone to help with computer stuff on the outside. Someone who nobody's going to be watching right now—which means, they can't be associated with our normal circle of friends at all."

Velma looked astonished, but not really. I mean, she knew how I thought. She'd probably figured it out almost as quickly as I had.

"Is your laptop in your bag?" I asked.

She was already digging it out.

"I wondered how long it would take for you to ask to check your email," she said.

Typing felt so weird. After your hands have been away from it, even for a little while, the keystrokes feel like a distant memory, like writing your name with crayons.

I logged on, and there was Matty, his name poised on my buddy list like he had nothing better to do with his life than wonder when I would leave my self-imposed mountain seclusion.

"Baby, you are such a sight for sore eyes," I typed, smiling shyly as I did.

"Hi Candy :)"

"Well, your screenname's a sight for sore eyes, anyway," I wrote, knowing Matty would dive right into the geek humor. "Tell me you've missed me?"

"Of course I have baby."

"Good. I've missed you, too."

"Where have you been?"

"Oh, you know, just here and there. What have you been up to?"

"Just school and stuff. But where are you???"

"You know I can't tell you that. But I've been wanting to talk to you so bad . . ."

"Just tell me where you are, then we can meet up and kiss :)"

Okay. One smiley-face emoticon in a conversation with Matty was weird enough. But, two? I didn't want to be that kind of girl, but this was not like the Matty I knew. It wasn't even like the Matty I almost knew.

"What's up, C?" said Velma, perking up next to me on the Land Rover.

"Matty's on. But . . ."

"But what?"

"It's not Matty."

Velma understood what I meant at once. "Are you sure?"

"Not totally sure. But something feels very wrong."

"Did he do that thing he did before?" Velma asked. "You know, where he told you where you were at? The computer should register as being in Atlanta, that's what Mr. Patterson set it for."

"Don't you know?" I typed back.

"Just tell me just for fun."

Velma was already fishing the gold phone out of her bag, dialing Matty's number. She handed it to me, pressed it up to my ear. It took a while to ring.

"You there?" said the Matty onscreen.

"Hey-lo," came Matty's voice, chirpily high-pitched through the phone receiver.

"Matty, it's Candy," I said. "I have something that might sound totally stupid. Am I talking to you online right now?"

"No way," he said. "I'm in—uh, I'm at work right now."

"Can you go to a computer?"

"Sure. What's up, babe?"

"There's somebody online," I said. "It says you're online, but it's not *you*. Does anyone else use your password?"

"No way. I mean, if they did, you would totally know."

"Can you get online and look?" I asked.

"Why? It's no big deal," Matty said. "Just don't talk to him."

I felt a lump in my throat. It felt like a confession. "I already am."

Something in my voice must have sounded dire. Matty was like, "Okay, give me one second," and I could hear his feet thudding down the hall, stammered explanations being made.

I handed the computer to Velma. "Keep typing. Pretend you're me," I whispered to her. "But don't let on that you know anything. And, for God's sake, don't tell him any information."

Velma nodded. She began typing at once.

"Okay, I'm online," said Matty. "Where have you been, anyway?"

"Don't ask," I said. "Look, I know this sounds crazy, but there's a man who wants to kill me and I think he's using your screen name."

All of a sudden, a weird beep came out of the computer and another chatting screen appeared, with the words WHAT'S UP VELMA! in three-inch high letters.

"Matty," I said into the phone, "that had better be you."

"Relax," he said. "It's my alternate screen name. I only use it for hacker chats and MUDding."

"You are *such* a geek."

"So look. Who's this guy who's using my screen name to put the moves on my girl?"

"Well, why don't you find out?" I said.

"Oh yeah. Yeah, I can do that." I heard quick, stabbing keystrokes over the phone. "Weird, it's a protected account. Okay, no problem, I can work around that . . ." He let out a low whistle. "This is some seriously pro-level work, Candy. Were you kidding about that wanting-to-kill-you bit?"

"Can you break in?" I asked, trying not to sound too desperate.

"Almost . . . *there*." A quick ding on Matty's side of the phone. "It looks like a hotel server. A hotel . . . right here, in New York. Actually, not too far from my apartment. You want the address?"

I thought for a moment. Velma looked up at me. "The guy on Matty's account is typing weird things," she said, pained. "I think he's onto us."

"Tell him you have to go," I said to Velma.

"Me?" squawked Matty over the phone.

"No," I said. "Matty, you just stay put. I think we're coming for a visit."

"A visit?" His voice cracked with fear.

"Don't worry," I said, trying to sound as reassuring and soothing as I could. "You are gonna be so safe, it's not funny. Just stick around. We'll be there in a day or so."

I hung up quickly. As soon as I did, Velma closed up her computer.

"What now?" she asked, looking at me hopefully.

"Now," I said, "we go see what's up in New York."

By midday, we had reached the bottom of the hill, and we'd entered into summer, too. The town swarmed with people, all wearing thin cotton coveralls, dealing admirably with the heat. In the village, children were cracking open juicy green fruits that looked like pineapples on the outside and kiwis on the inside, and tasted warm and sugary. We stopped to buy two, and after a brief period of debate—were they dangerous? were we hungry? dehydrated?—we ate them straight from the shell. I swear we were really learning how to live.

Soupha let us off way farther down than he should have, when night was over and the dawn was just beginning to crack. The ground had changed from snow to hard foliage, leafy Cretaceous plants and knots of wood that were multiple yards in diameter. Velma had peeled away her anorak, sweaters, and shirt to boy-beater level, and as she fiddled with that, wondering whether she should freeball in her sports bra, I could see Soupha looking a little hot under the toga. "That's the village right down there," I said. "I'm sure we could walk the rest of it."

Soupha, who definitely looked like he could use a rest—both Velma and I had slept on the Land Rover; he hadn't even stirred from his seat—nodded courteously, offered once more to take us the rest of the way, but I thanked him and declined. "Soupha," I said, "you are *so* one of the good guys, you know?"

He shrugged. "Just doing my job."

"Well, rock on."

"Uh, right." He put the Land Rover in reverse, plowing right back up the way he'd come.

I never understood guys like that. They're so anxious to get you somewhere, and as soon as you finally get there, the first thing they want to do is head back.

The Reunion That Wasn't

(13)

We stopped by Velma's hotel room to get our luggage. Then we took the world's slowest taxi into Bangkok. When we got there at dusk, the city looked like a series of glowing towers in the middle of a flat plateau of desert, and then we flew into New York, which made Bangkok's skyscraper-stacked skyline look like a desert.

The plane landed at La Guardia early in the snowy morning. It was usually my favorite time of day in New York, when I'd wake up earlier than everyone else and slip out of our hotel room and take the elevator down to the street. The streets always seemed to be flushed with people, and I loved to watch them, but best of all was when only a few people were on the streets, the strange old men who always woke up the earliest, and all the construction workers who stared at me, as though they were invisible and I couldn't see them. I liked staring back. It made them so nervous when I did that that they stared straight at the ground. It was all part of the games I played.

And I don't mean to be such a pushover, but right now I could never play another mind game on anyone again and I would be perfectly fine with that.

I didn't know what was the matter with me. I was supposed to be jubilant and buggy. I was about to meet the boy I'd been crushing on. The boy I'd evaded death for.

Instead, I watched gloomily as Velma made up dorky synchronized dances to the techno song that was on the cab radio.

"You kids come here a lot?" the cabbie shouted at us through the Plexiglas barricade between the front and rear seats.

"Uh, we live here," I called back at him. "On the Upper West Side. And don't call us kids."

The driver glanced through the rearview mirror at Velma doing the Fishy Swim. "Right, okay then," he said, turning back to the road.

We pulled up around the corner from Matty's apartment building, a posh high-rise on Riverside Drive. The doorman was a distinguished-looking Sikh man with a high white turban and a bowtie. When Velma stripped out of her anorak—I was wearing my simple Jill Stuart sweater dress—he let us in without calling up. The lobby had several hanging gold-plated chandeliers. This was utterly the kind of building my father's friends used to live in. God. The past tense was already starting to kick in. I stifled it; there were too many other things going on for me to stop going now.

"Does Matty do that well at the magazine?" I whispered to Velma.

"Maybe he comes from high breeding," she whispered back.

"Maybe he never left," I said, as three couples, all straddling the border between middle-aged and taxidermied, crowded onto the elevator with us. One of the husbands checked me out. I smiled to his wife sympathetically, and stepped on his toe as we walked out.

"Do I look chipper?" I asked Velma in the hallway.

"You look . . . less depressed?"

"Do I?" I chirped, not unhappily.

"Determined. You look determined. How does that sound?"

"I could be satisfied with 'determined,'" I said. We stopped in front of the room number Matty had given us.

His surname was on the doorbell.

I felt my stomach jump.

I rang the bell, at first timidly and then again, with an explosion of self-confidence, holding in the button for an obscene amount of time.

A middle-aged woman pulled open the door.

She stared at us, obviously irritated at our presence. "Can I help you?" she asked icily, her eyes darting to my finger, which was still pressing the buzzer in.

I pulled my finger back, feeling my cheeks swell up crimson.

Velma stepped in front, lightly elbowing me aside. Her voice snapped into her full-on affected Old South accent. "I'm sorry, ma'am, I do believe we probably have the wrong number," she said. "My sister and I were just looking for our friend Matty's residence, I sure do regret the bother, we'll be on our way."

The woman's eyes flickered from my face, moved down and left, and lingered on Velma. If I didn't know better, I would have thought she was sizing us up.

But my eyes swept over the apartment inside. Fuzzy, tall white rugs, tables and cabinets made of glass and Czech crystal. A winding spiral staircase that led to an ornate second floor. The walls were paneled with expensive-looking mahogany, and chandeliers hung in every room.

"Uh, Mom," came a voice—a male voice—and the racket of feet pounded down the metal steps of the staircase. "I think it might be my . . ."

The boy started down the staircase, bouncing on the carpeted steps. He froze on the stairs as soon as he saw us.

And he turned as white as the stripes of my dress.

The boy was wearing floppy skater jeans and a cheesy, cartoon-illustrated They Might Be Giants T-shirt. Hi-top Converse shoes, a worn-out shade of black, with song lyrics scribbled in black Sharpie pen along the tips and sides. His auburn hair stood in messy spikes that signified beyond definitely that he for sure *was* a boy, a few strands sticking up at his cowlick, and his glossy doe-blue eyes widened. Freckles dotted his just-barely-pubescing face.

"Oh," he croaked.

The woman at the door turned to him, puzzled. "Do you know these people?" she asked.

"Hi, Velma. Hi, Candy," said the boy, shakily, in that now-familiar voice.

That abnormally high, always-about-to-crack wobbly voice.

My cheeks flamed up even more. I felt like a cross between a funeral march and a falling anvil.

Velma just rested one hand on one hip and cocked her head.

She smiled suavely.

"Hi, Matty," she said.

Matty took us upstairs, to his room, and we decompressed. First, though, his mom took Velma's anorak and both of our boots to dry off in the kitchen, and offered me a robe to change into so I could get out of my soaking wet dress—which was not bothering me, because nothing made me uncomfortable anymore, but it was dripping with slush, too much to walk around the house in.

"Well, ladies," Matty announced, "welcome to my bedroom."

"Matty," I said. "Would you mind leaving us alone for a second?"

"Sure," said Matty, looking even more small and scared every minute. He backed away quickly toward the door of his bedroom, slipped out through its narrow crevice, and slammed it shut so that only the oh-so-MTV poster of Jimmy Eat World stared back at us.

"Oh my God," I said. "Oh my God."

"Um," said Velma, "wow."

"Oh my God oh my God ohmygod. Oh. My. Whoa, Velma. This is *so* seriously perturbing."

"You mean, *dis*turbing?"

"No, *per*turbing, 'cause we both must be seriously perturbed. How old is he, like, ten?"

"Thirteen, at least."

"And you've been talking to him forever. And *I*— well, yeah, and I have been more than just *talk*ing to him. I am a total perturbvert. I can't believe this, I just can*not* believe this. I mean—*any* of it. But especially now, especially *this*, I just can't believe—"

Velma's voice cut through the air. It cut my ears, and then it cut me, quick and sharp like a whip.

"Fuck that," she said.

My eyes widened. I looked up in surprise at little Velma, who still blushed when she said *sex*.

"What?"

Velma stood up in front of me, all five feet and one inch of her. Her hands rested on her hips. Her eyes were like firecrackers.

"You. You and your disbelief. You're always like, 'I can't believe this' and 'I don't believe you.' Well, I just said *fuck that* because, Candy, honey, you need to shut the fuck up. You need to stop evaluating your surroundings for one second, and just *live* in them. You have got to start believing all this messed-up stuff, even if it is messed up, because, it is happening."

I listened to her, and I totally understood every word she said.

And then we both froze.

Outside the room, we could hear footsteps. The footsteps grew closer. They stopped just outside the door, in surprise. You could hear the questioning in them as they halted so suddenly. And then Matty's mother's voice, crisp and direct as a football umpire: "Matty, why are you standing outside your own room?"

We shot alarmed, indecisive looks at each other.

"My friends—uh, they wanted to freshen up or do some girl stuff or something. They just got in from far away," he said.

"Where do you know them from?"

Velma's fingers wrapped around my hand. She squeezed tight.

Matty's hesitation was slim to not at all. His voice dipped into a story that was long, involved, boring, and—most crucial of all—sounded absolutely true.

Velma and I stared at each other, wide-eyed, incredulous.

There was a knock on the door. It had been so long since someone had just knocked on a door and waited for us to say "come in" that we'd almost forgotten to say it. Velma recovered before I did, and the door clicked open.

Matty waded in. His mother stood at the door, still checking us out.

"Matty, did you ask your friends if they'd like to have a shower?" Matty's mom asked.

I looked at Velma and Matty, standing in the doorway to his room, all four of their eyes about to bug out of their skulls with surprise and incredulity.

I flashed a delighted look at her, one girl to another.

"Actually," I said, "that would be wonderful."

And I left Matty and Velma to negotiate their own way through this weirdness.

Meanwhile, I retreated to the familiar confines of a bathroom, because no matter what country or culture you're in, you can always hide out inside a bathroom. I closed the door behind me and locked myself in, stripping off my robe, jumping inside that glass chamber of a shower in Matty's parents' bedroom. There were pictures in that bedroom, all over the place, of

Matty as a child. Well, as an even younger child. That same baggy T-shirt, that same expression, those big doe eyes, like a deer caught in headlights. Man, was I going to give him some headlights to get caught in.

But as soon as the hot droplets of water started to hit my body, I relaxed. I felt stress shoot out of me like hiccups escaping, and the tightness of my spine sizzled and dropped away.

This was the first time I'd been alone, I mean, *really* alone, since I'd left Handler in Prague. Mr. Patterson. The monks. Velma. I'd spent so much time keeping up appearances. Every time I talked to someone else now, it felt like an act. All I really wanted to talk about was my father, and I covered that up by thinking about revenge, and I covered that up by talking about innocuous things so nobody knew what I was really thinking about.

And I still didn't know how to get past this. I still kept feeling this urge to call my father, tell him I was still in hiding, but no, I'm fine and it's all going to be over soon. And I still felt like I needed to dig out my books and study more, but I hadn't seen my school books since—when? San Francisco? Mr. Patterson's head-quarters?—I didn't even remember.

Cities melting into each other used to be a sign of a really good modeling season, or Velma throwing a tantrum with her credit cards. Now, it made me feel old and weathered, like I couldn't remember where I'd been or when or what city I was in the last time I spoke to my father. Christ, what had I even said? "Hi Daddy, I'm missing my labs and running around the world, but don't worry, it'll be over before you know it?"

I probably hadn't even remembered to tell him I missed him. With one final, violent shudder, all that weight in my spine flowed back and I was tense, again, more tense than before, like bricks.

It'll be over before you know it.

That was all I could hang onto right now.

I snapped off the water valve. I dried off quickly, wrapped the towel around me, and went in search of my dress.

Matty and Velma were still sitting in his room. Neither was saying anything. Velma sat on the side of Matty's bedspread. Matty faced her, his legs dangling down, almost reaching the floor. His hands hung helplessly between his knees. They were staring at each other, eyes locked. What's more, they were actually the same height.

When I walked in, wearing my now dry dress, both of their heads immediately snapped toward me.

I shook out my hair, brushed it back with a hand, and plopped down on the bed opposite Velma.

"So, um," Velma fished, anxious to break the silence. "Maybe I should hop in the shower now."

She bounced off the bed, jumped up, and nearly lunged out of that room, slamming the door behind her. I felt a sudden impulse to grab her by her messy blond ponytail and hold her in front of me as camouflage, or as support, as a way to get away.

But the door clicked shut.

And then it was just me and Matty.

I knew I didn't want to be the first one to talk. I wasn't feeling tricked or duped or anything. I was feeling like I should have realized, and feeling like he hadn't been doing anything wrong and I just hadn't bothered to ask, "How old are you?"

But also, I'd never told him that I was in Europe or that Velma was a billionaire or that his life was in danger. And that really *was* all my fault. I could have stopped talking to him until it settled down. I could have not used traceable credit cards to check my email.

But no—I had to be so egotistical. I had to stay in Rome and play around while Preston killed my dad.

"Wow," Matty said, still staring at me with that big-eyed television gleam. "Candy. Damn. Um, hi."

I kept staring back at him. I didn't say a word.

Matty flinched awkwardly.

"So," he offered, by way of making conversation, "I guess you really aren't a forty-year-old man."

"Yeah," I said. "Apparently, neither are you."

I arched one eyebrow. Another blank space.

Another silence.

"I'm sorry about your father," said Matty.

I looked up in surprise. "How did you know?"

He gave me a big *duh* look. "I'm a hacker, remember? Your last name was easy. Then I saw him on the news, and—shit, I'm sorry, am I saying something wrong? I've just never had to, you know—"

"You don't have to do anything," I said.

"I know," he said. "But I want to."

My lower lip trembled. I was so close to spilling it again, to losing it. He reached over and held my hand. I know he wasn't that much younger than me, but his hand was smaller than mine and it felt really weird and my hand jerked away, an automatic reaction. We looked at each other. He looked afraid. I was startled.

Then we both started laughing.

And, God, it felt so good to laugh.

"What *is* your deal, anyway?" I asked, shaking my head, as we both coughed and gasped for breath. "You're really him?"

Matty looked down into his hands. "I'm older than I look," he offered meekly.

"Do you really write for a magazine?"

"I do write," he said. "Mostly when I'm bored at work. Which is after school, in a magazine stand."

"But the rest of it was . . ."

"Yeah." Matty waited for a second. "But you're really a supermodel?"

"I don't know if I'm necessarily super. Right now I feel pretty damn ordinary. And I haven't felt like a model in about a million years. Mostly I just feel like people pay me to be blond. And my hair has been so greasy lately, I'm not even *that* very much anymore. I haven't really felt like anything since Rome . . . maybe even since San Francisco."

"Rome?"

"Oh yeah. Rome came, uh, after San Francisco but before Laos."

"Candy," Matty said, and I could see him desperately trying not to wig out and remind me that I was mentally insane, "what's been happening to you?"

"I was stalked," I told him. "I had to get away, and I think I'm getting better now, but weird things are happening to my body. I'm not even sure if I understand them. But in the meantime, he's still after me."

"No," Matty said. "I mean—what *happened*?"

"Oh," I stared at Matty. I realized just how in the dark we'd been keeping him. And so I told him everything, the whole story, from that first cosmetics shoot, the Men in Black in my bedroom, the chase, my fatal screw-up in Prague. Everything, right up to and including the monastery and our flying here. Matty took it in, not interrupting me at all, his eyes growing wider with every plane flight.

Finally, I finished, and we sat there in silence.

"Yes," I said at last.

"Yes what?"

"Yes there is something you can do for me. Be my friend."

"What, like, say that I'm your friend if that guy calls my house?"

"No. Velma always talks about how she can never keep boys as friends—like, she always ends up hooking up with them. I don't even have that problem. I never let anyone inside in the first place."

"But you let me in . . . ."

"I guess you didn't feel real at the time," I said. "And you seem like just the right kind of guy."

"I do?"

"For a just-friend, I mean."

I flashed him a smile. And, for the first time in a long time, I meant it.

Velma popped in just then, back in her jeans and sweater again. She pulled on her blazer from before, but she looked remarkably brighter, like her personality had gotten airbrushed. She hopped to Matty's desk and sat herself down next to the computer.

"So this is where you talk to us from?" she asked.

"Yeah!" said Matty, full of energy when it came to talking about computers. "I just upgraded my system with a new sound card. Now, when I send messages, it plays New Wave music in the key of whatever you type. Bad news—sounds like metal songs."

His hands scampered toward his computer, and his feet perched on the edge of his swivel chair.

"Matty," I said. "Excuse us."

"Sure," said Matty, voice wavering.

I grabbed Velma's arm. I pulled her into me and put my lips against her ear.

"What do you think?" I whispered. "Is this another part of Preston's trap? Should I cut the flow of oxygen to his brain?"

Velma heaved a sigh of exasperation straight into my ear.

"Candy," she said, "read the *signs*. His dorky T-shirts. His geeky computer setup. The fact that he hacked the *Family* in under five minutes. Right now, we are not in much of a position to choose our allies. And this is a kid—alright, a kid, but still—someone who *wants* to be our ally."

I sat.

I thought.

I was feeling too extreme to make any real judgment calls, but I did anyway. There was one thing I knew for sure: when this was over, I was going to take a long, long break from dating.

"Okay," I said out loud.

"Okay?" asked Velma.

"Okay?" asked Matty.

"Okay. Let's do this. Velma—Preston is probably still in New York, right?"

"Probably," Velma said.

I nodded.

"So let's kick his ass."

"Okay," she agreed brightly, nodding.

"Matty," I said, "how old are you?"

Matty opened his mouth wide to protest. I swear I thought he was going to *"I thought you knew!"* me. "Don't," I snapped, and his mouth closed immediately.

"Fourteen. And a half."

"Holy shit."

Matty waited a second, and then added: "But I'm very mature for my age."

"I have no doubt," I said. "The question is, how good are you?"

"Candy!" Velma scolded.

"Not like *that*," I groaned. I walked over to Matty, took him by the shoulders, plopped him in the computer chair, and swiveled him around. "How *good*. I want you to find out everything you can about Preston Reign."

Matty hit the space bar on his computer.

"What, like, that cosmetics guy? You just Google him, there's like a million articles. Fan sites, too, probably. What do you want to know?"

"Where was the last time he used his credit card?"

Matty swallowed.

"Well," he said, "that's not gonna be on Google."

I shrank away from the computer. I stared out the window at nothing. Matty's fingers sounded like raindrops as he typed. It was the exact sound of my despair sinking in.

"Sedgewick Hotel," he announced, reading as the words sprung up on the monitor. "That's a couple of blocks up from here."

Velma and I gave a start.

Matty shrugged, broadcasting innocence.

"I didn't say Google was all I had," he offered.

I stared at Matty—and then I stared *past* Matty, at the hotel's font on his computer. The sturdy, unforgiving type dripped expensive and classy.

He was here.

I felt a surge of adrenaline hit as I touched the logo. I strode across the room, slipped on my heels, and reached for—what? something? I looked at Velma, momentarily shaken. I really felt like I'd forgotten something. Only, I didn't wear jackets anymore. And my suitcase, I could leave here.

"What's wrong?" said Velma.

I shook my head. "Nothing, I guess. I'm ready. I'm set. I'm going."

"Do you want this?" Velma's hand offered nothing, but her fingers traced the almost-not-there outline of the gun in her pocket.

I considered, then shook my head. "It would only slow me down," I said.

"Okay," Velma shrugged. "Let's go."

That's what I was hesitating about. That's what I wasn't sure if I had.

Velma.

I wanted to argue with her, to tell her to stay home, out of the line of fire, that she'd just be a dead weight. I knew she wouldn't. God knows what she could do, but I didn't even think to question whether or not she was coming.

She was.

Matty hurried alongside us, running to keep up. We marched out of his room and down the stairs. We passed Matty's mom in the hallway, who looked as though she still hadn't recovered from the shock of seeing two eighteen-year-old girls storming into her barely teenage son's room. Matty waved good-bye to her, walked us to the elevator, and got in with us.

"You know, Matty, you don't need to walk us out," I said.

"I'm not walking you out. I'm going in with you."

"What a coincidence," I said, "that's exactly what you're *not* doing."

"Look," said Matty. He shifted the weight of his computer, tucked under his arm. "I've been sitting on the sidelines for so long I've got a crease in my ass from it. And I think, with the amount of waiting I've done, I think the least I deserve is a piece of the action."

"Are you crazy?" Velma said. "We're going to get killed!"

Both Matty and I shot evil glares at her, *I can't believe you said that*.

"Okay," I said. "You can come. But only because I need to prove Velma wrong."

The elevator clunked, and the doors slid open.

The three of us walked out, stormed past the doorman, threw open the main doors, and went out into the frozen New York street.

"Now where?" I said.

"I *told* you you needed me," Matty said. He gestured with his computer. "Two blocks that way."

The street was busy for this time of day. Cars whizzed by in slow motion, flashes of yellow and orange against the milky black asphalt. People pushed past each other, bundled up in coats and scarves and hats, so many layers that they looked like bumper cars, jostling into each other as they moved.

We turned in the direction that Matty pointed.

And then, a strange thing happened.

Everybody on the street stopped.

Tall skinny homeless people, big fat businessmen on the way home from work, kids slipping across the icy sidewalk with one hand affixed to their nannies' gloves. The cars along the street all stopped, all the cars in both directions, not even bothering to pull into parking spots. The drivers all climbed out.

Every driver—every driver on that entire street—was carrying a shotgun.

The businessmen opened their briefcases and pulled out guns.

The homeless people opened their umbrellas and pulled out guns.

The doormen and nannies and the little grade-school kids, too, the nondescript old ladies walking poodles let go of the leashes and let the poodles scurry down the sidewalk, in search of whatever meaty-smelling New York bistro they were yipping about—all of them stopped what they were doing, however they were undercover, and then they were holding guns.

And all those guns were trained on me.

The car that had stopped right in front of Matty's family's building—a sleek black European affair that you wouldn't have thought was a limousine, but up close now seemed to be exactly that, swung its back door open.

Preston stepped out.

"Darling," he said, a stir of bravado in his voice. "What a pleasant surprise."

Behind me, the cabbie from earlier poked me in the back with a .22 assault rifle.

I whipped my hand around, caught it, and gave it a rough jostle. The gun fell to the ground.

Which meant there were only about two hundred guns still pointing at me.

"This is totally what the abbot talked about," I said. When I spoke, my eyes never left Preston. "Illusions. Fakery. He said never to be fooled by the veils. You—this whole thing—it's all one big charade, isn't it?"

Preston spoke again. This time his voice whipped harshly, like the wind.

"I have no idea what you're talking about," he said. "You may put on a fancy show, but you can't outrun bullets. Not this many. Not even if you *are* a ninja."

He leaned closer, close enough for me to smell his cologne, even with the million cold smells of a New York winter. "Which, I really should tell you," he whispered confidentially, "I find very, *very* sexy."

He pulled back.

"Let the two children go," he announced. "If I touch the girl, I might actually have to answer to someone, and I suspect that eliminating the boy will be more trouble than he's worth."

His eyes flickered back to me.

"And, as for you, Candy," he crooned—sounding so sweet, it was sickening—

And then he knocked me out.

Heroes & Villains

(14)

I woke up with salt air crawling through my nostrils like worms, my head aching like a hangover, and my mouth dry as sandpaper. The skin on my body tingled, a peculiar sensation of being cold and hot at the same time. My first thought was, I was staying in a hotel in Europe and I'd left the heater and the A.C. both turned on by accident.

My second thought—as I opened my eyes, seeing nothing but the wide and distant sea, glistening blue—was, at least I had a room with a view.

"Wakey, wakey," sang a voice from behind me. A voice I knew all too well.

I blinked a bunch of times, scratched my nose, and roused myself from the gravel.

Preston was sitting in a green and pink striped beach chair, perched on a crag of rock a few feet away from me.

"And how *is* my little red-hot sack of dynamite this morning?" he asked.

My eyes darted around, looking for the aforementioned dynamite.

Preston chuckled. "No, no," he said. "I was only paying you a compliment. How thoughtless of me. Oh well—as a suitor, I guess I do tend toward extremes, wouldn't you say?"

There was a curious plodding-ness to his words, like he'd thought of them a long time ago and was just spitting them out of his mouth like trite old movie lines. I wondered if he still really cared about this, me rejecting him and getting even and taking out his revenge, or if his feelings had run their course and now he was just going through the motions.

Then I thought of my father, and I remembered that I wasn't going to let that bastard go more than five feet without nailing his arms onto a crucifix.

I stood, still wobbly, and a fast soft tropical wind coasted over my skin and into my hair. Still the sensation of extreme hot and extreme cold. I was standing on a narrow cliff. We both were. To my left was a sharply receding cliff, almost vertical. Behind Preston sat an empty helicopter, the one he must have flown us here in. To my right was a pool of throbbing opaque liquid that glowed a dull orange red. I'd never seen one up close before, but it looked too familiar to not know what it was. Too much like the pictures they showed us in school and on those NOVA programs on public TV that my father used to watch.

It was a volcano.

We were standing on the edge of a volcano.

Preston stood, grabbed my arm, and pulled me close. He dug his gun into my lungs. The air was hazy, smoky. Lava spurted from the canyon in small, bare farts of molten rock.

He repeated himself in small words.

"Date! Me! Or! Die!"

He peered at me like he actually expected an answer. I wondered if he was dumbing down the question because I was blond, or for his own edification.

"So you're, like, going to sacrifice me to a volcano?" I asked disbelievingly. I mean, I knew he was obsessive, but I didn't think it was to the extent of idolatry.

He smiled coyly. "No," he said. "If you turn me down, though, it *is* an easy cleanup. Mostly, I just like the view."

"You really *are* the most self-obsessed man on the planet," I said.

That made him chuckle. God, do you think some people just, like, know intrinsically that they're evil? He played into the role so well. "You're so right," he demurred. "But, then again—wouldn't you be, if you were me? I swear, they should make me into a reality show."

I groaned.

"And, by the way," he said, "don't even bother trying to attack me. This gun's not going anywhere."

"Right," I rolled my eyes. "Because, like, I thought you might give your gun a coffee break."

He moved the gun from my lungs and shoved it into my stomach. He hit the area right beneath my ribs. My stomach lurched, and I felt a sudden impulse to vomit, but I held it in. I gritted my teeth. I struggled, digging my heels into the volcano dirt, trying to steady myself.

"There's still time to change your mind," he said. "I was insulted by how you turned me down before, in your bedroom, you know."

"You were *insulted*?"

"Well, it *was* your fault. And I was definitely hurt. Want to kiss and make it better?"

The gun in my ribs relaxed, but not enough. Preston's face came close to mine. His lips quivered. For one dangerous second, I could feel myself pulling in, considering it, really thinking about it. He was not an ugly man. He was handsome, rich, good-smelling, well-connected. With a snap of his fingers, he could have me out of this mess, and I would never be on the run again.

I reminded myself: He was also totally insane.

A spurt of lava knocked us both off our feet. The heat alone was what bowled us over. The lava flew out of the pit and cut the air at a wide, even angle, dangerously close to us. The heat burned the air around us like a hot kettle pressed against our entire bodies. It was like an invisible bubble of fire.

I hustled to get back up. Preston was quick, too. I hooked my fingers between jutting bits of rock and pulled myself steady, then scrambled to my feet. By the time I was standing, though, he was too, training his gun ominously in my direction.

"That wasn't your fault, Candy," he said, roaring. "I'm not going to shoot you for that."

I wasn't paying attention to what he said, as he rambled on. I couldn't pay attention.

I was too busy counting.

Preston saw my lips moving. Abruptly, he broke off.

"What are you doing?" he snarled.

The gun jutted into my ribs.

Twenty-one Mississippi, twenty-two Mississippi . . .

The magma droplet splashed into the ocean.

"I'm not going to ask you again," Preston sneered. At this moment, he looked uglier than he ever had. His face was distorted, muscles twisted like a crying baby.

My eyes darted down to the water.

"What?" Preston demanded, following the trail of my glance.

There was a sizzle from far below for four-Mississippi seconds more. Then the blast of gas released, a cone of steam shot up from beneath the water, and the surface of the ocean exploded like a bubbling fountain.

Twenty-six Mississippi.

"I don't like the way your eyes are moving. It feels too much like you're planning something, honey," he said, milking that word *honey* for all the sentimental value he could squeeze. It wasn't a lot. The gun pressed farther into my ribcage. I winced as the metal bit into my flesh.

"Tell me what you're thinking!" he screamed, suddenly unhinged.

I wondered if this was the mark of truly insane people, how they can seem cold and calculated one minute and like wild animals the next. My silence was making him nervous. He regarded it as the implied threat of escape. Of me figuring out how to make it past him, snatch the gun, pickpocket his keys, and make it back into his private chopper.

When, really, salvation was going to be as quick as throwing myself off a cliff.

The next bolt of magma was small, too small. It streamed between us like a figure brushing by. I shook, but he didn't. I didn't have to appear composed. He did. He was waiting for my answer.

The answer.

He was counting down the seconds that I had to live.

"Ten. Nine . . ."

I realized—if I wasn't lucky—he really *would* be counting down the seconds I had left.

"Eight. Seven."

"God, you're counting so slow. I never told you, Preston, but your voice is like a TV weatherman . . . ."

He kept going like I didn't say anything.

"Six. Five. Four."

And I smiled.

I smiled because I heard a rumbling.

And I knew what that rumbling meant.

"What the *hell* are you smiling at, Candy? If you don't tell me, forget the countdown, I'll throw you into the pit myself."

The magma bubbled louder.

"Now why would you do that, Preston? You'd lose your perfect sense of timing."

The next bolt that shot out our way was almost exactly the same size as the first one, maybe a little smaller. I started counting. Preston, no longer interested in my lips, started counting too.

"Four."

four Mississippi

"Three."

three Mississippi

"Two."

two Mississippi

"Two and one-half . . ."

How did I know that Preston would be the type of guy to count two and a half? I was that kind of girl.

A lucky girl.

one Mississippi

I smiled, possibly the most charming smile I have afforded anyone in I can't remember how long. I slipped off my shoes.

"Good-bye, Preston," I whispered sweetly.

And I threw myself off the volcano.

I jumped. My bare feet pressed against rock, finding the strongest foothold in that uneven ground, crafted as much by wind and erosion as by the primordial fires that first formed the volcano thousands of years ago. I pushed off with my heels, arched my body like a rainbow, and cut the air with my arms angled straight, hands spread, as symmetrical as hands can ever be, lying directly on top of one another. I aimed my body as close to that glowing drop of red molten rock as I could.

I let myself drop.

The air hammered closed all around me. I never felt gravity so hard, pounding on my skin like a personal vendetta. I kept my body packed as thin as falling free will allow, which, let me tell you, isn't so free. With nothing at all to hold onto for miles and no ground around, it was almost impossible to make yourself move and fight against the deafening rush of air and grit your teeth and *just will* your legs closer together. Maybe I shouldn't have jumped headfirst. I was almost surely going to break something on impact.

But if everything went right, when I made contact, I was going to need my legs more.

I braced myself for the oncoming—

CONTACT

—and then I connected with the water.

The pain was sharper than I expected, a loud pain, not like getting punched so much as getting a needle rammed through your body. I tried to roll over, to upright myself underwater. I closed my eyes and pretended I didn't just hear that loud pop in my shoulder and pretended the water wasn't pounding my body from every side, fighting against the natural inclination of my skeleton to stay together and not collapse right now—

WHOOM

—the gas bubble hit me and flipped me and sent me crashing to the surface, and then sent me crashing *through* the surface, and I was surrounded by air again, flying ten feet above the face of the ocean and my head was tipped back and my lips were sucking in air, eating up that oxygen like I couldn't get enough. And my legs were still kicking, paddling my fall back down in the direction of land, and I hopped and flopped back into the water, and when I had fallen in up to my knees, another burst of gas came from another blob of lava, bouncing me back up into the air. I played hopscotch this way, riding the gas bubbles until the trail fizzled out, an easy swim from land.

That's about the time I realized my right shoulder was dislocated.

I got to shore by a combination of kicking and one-handed dog paddle. Just as I was about to collapse, the current caught me. I landed on the shore and flopped over on my back, coughing fitfully, trying to finally lie down and stop my body from shaking so hard. It wouldn't.

Finally, I pulled myself up, got to my knees shakily, and looked around.

With my left hand, the arm that still worked, I pulled my dress down. It was even less of a dress now than when I'd bought it. Which was saying a lot. If there was anyone alive around, they were almost certainly getting a free show. Only I don't think there was.

The sun was still out, gleaming bright and tropical. I rubbed my eyes.

Voices. Words that were still too mushed together to understand.

Images began to fade in. Velma. Matty. At first they seemed like the same face, then two different faces, wobbling in and out of each other.

Now the words were clearing up.

"Can I give her mouth-to-mouth?"

"Only if you want your teeth ripped out, kiddo," said Velma, elbowing him out of the way.

Both of their profiles slowly faded into view. Matty was looking a little worse for wear, like someone had socked him in the stomach. Velma had a great big shiner of a bruise over her left eye. I blinked, then wheezed, coughing water out of my lungs, then watching as Matty and Velma's anxious and worried and happy faces popped into my blurred vision like holograms.

"What's going on?" I croaked out.

"Come on, girl," said Velma. "I don't know how much time we have, but it can't be a lot."

"My shoulder," I said.

"What?" Velma asked, peering at my oddly twisted right arm.

"I need you to fix it."

"I can't fix your shoulder!" she cried.

"Relax," said Matty. "I'll look it up online."

"You can do it on the helicopter. Now, move," said Velma firmly, motioning us along.

"One second," I said. I bent down, knelt on a rock, and puked up the entire contents of my stomach. Then I rose, dusted my knees off, thankfully noted the lack of vomit on myself, and hurried after Velma into her small private helicopter.

Good Vibrations

(15)

Being in New York was comforting. The streets were calm, in that reassuring order so you know 84th Street follows 83rd, and that Macy's, Barney's, and Times Square will always be right where you left them.

We took a cab straight to Matty's place, breezed past his mother (whose half-casual "Why aren't you in school?" went totally unheeded) and up the stairs. We stood in our freshly changed clothes, crowded around Matty's computer, and stared at the monitor.

Matty's fingers swam over the keys. We watched the connection, the sign-in screen, the buddy list . . . .

"It's no good," Matty said. "His name is turning up gray. That means he's not online."

"So, what, we're supposed to just wait for him to come on?"

Matty shrugged. "Unless you can psychically *pull* him online."

Velma would not take it sitting down. "There must be *something* you can do," she said. "Trace his screen name. Email him, for God's sake—anything! We *know* he's out there! We know his tricks, don't we? Why can't we do anything?"

"I really don't know what to do," he whined, that fourteen-year-old inexperience creeping into his voice.

"It didn't stop you from finding all those nekkid pictures of Candy, did it?" Velma threw her hands in the air in exasperation.

"Quiet," I said.

I breathed in and listened, ignoring the pain in my shoulder. The crisp snowy air. The fir trees in Riverside Park, with their wintergreen leaves and urine-spattered bark. Car exhaust on Cathedral Parkway, a thousand motorists' hearts pounding with impatient arrogance. My eyes were glazing over. My breathing got heavier.

"She's lost it," Matty whispered. "If she loses it, we've lost the whole game."

"We're not losing," Velma said.

I breathed deeper.

On West End Avenue, a woman the age my mother would have been walked her dog, her insulated workout suit soaking with sweat, leash wrapped several times around her hand. Her breathing and the dog's were totally synchronous. In the gold-plated penthouse of Trump Tower, a lonely, gray-haired millionaire brought a steak knife down into steak, the sinews of meat parting under the blade. On the corner of 73rd and Broadway, a Hasidic Jew my age, his beard down to his stomach, played Eddie Cantor and Green Day songs on an acoustic guitar, collecting nickels and quarters from yuppie couples on dinner dates.

"Maybe he just hasn't gotten back yet?" whispered Matty.

Closer, I told myself. My own pulse pounded in my ears like it was going to explode.

On the second floor of this building, a cranky man microwaved his dinner. The unmistakable smell of inflating pasta and powdered cheddar cheese hit my nose, reminding me of Velma's sorority house back in Atlanta. Two blocks away, a twelve-year-old girl plucked her eyebrows for the first time. A woman toweling off after a shower. A man scratching a lottery ticket.

My eyes snapped open.

"Try his name again," I said. "He's here."

Matty clicked on the light gray screen name, the made-up word I'd met him under so many weeks ago. My heart was pounding now just as hard as it was pounding then.

Matty tried entering something on his keyboard. He frowned, typed some more.

"He's here," he said at last. "He's totally online, using my screen name. He's just set the program so that the name appears to be offline . . . damn, can you even do that? I guess you can."

Velma stopped sorting through her suitcase. "I don't get it. You can hack into people's bank accounts, but you don't know how to work Instant Messaging?"

Matty shrugged. "Sue me. Usually I'm just role-playing."

"Geez. It's almost like you were never one of the popular kids."

Matty flashed Velma a look that made her feel horrible and stupid. His eyes left the computer, but his fingers never did, and within seconds a location had popped right up. This time, Matty wasn't pulling any punches: it was a GPS coordinate, one that landed him right on the top floor of the Excelsior. He pulled up schematics of the hotel from a window on his computer screen that said SEDGEWICK HOTEL—INTERNAL MAINFRAME and counted off square feet.

"I've got him," Matty said. "He's in the penthouse. Of course."

We ran into his hallway and took the stairs at the rear of the building, feeling an eerie déjà vu about it.

"Look at it this way," Velma whispered. "After that last time, there's no way he can surprise us with anything."

It was no joke: as we snuck out the side door, the garage entrance that usually only the cleaning staff used, all our pulses raced faster, each one-upping the others as we got closer and closer to the outside.

Once we reached the door, we went out in reverse order—Matty, then Velma, then me. By now, Preston's men would probably recognize all of us, but there was the least chance of recognizing Matty. On the street, people had their collars turned up, faces layered with scarves. The wind chill that night was bitter, so much worse than Atlanta ever dreamed of.

"Do you see anyone?" I whispered to Matty.

"Left," he said back in a normal tone of voice.

I turned left. A man in a dark suit was dialing a number on his cell phone. I walked straight up to him, making eye contact like I was going to ask him a question. The man's eyes went wide with fear and confusion. I guess spying on someone and having them see you was like having the people on TV watch you back.

He was caught completely off guard, his dialing finger frozen in the air. I raised a hand to his shoulder. I sank my thumb and index finger to his neck, cut the blood flow to his head, and his body sunk against the pavement.

"Nice," said Matty.

"Good eye," I told him, squeezing his forearm. "Now, let's go."

Matty wasn't kidding, the hotel really was only a few blocks away. This time, we used the front door. Preston's men were all over the lobby, of course, but they weren't expecting us to walk right in. Two of them sat in the burgundy sofas, slumped and watching TV. One stood by the door with a radio cord in his ear. Another was at the checkout desk in the lobby, arguing over room service charges with the clerk on duty.

Room service charges. That meant they were getting ready to move.

That meant we had to move fast.

I strode past them, chin high, not even registering that I knew they were there. It seemed to work—they didn't make a move to change the channel, let alone to get up and attack us. This could only be regarded as a good sign.

We passed the concierge, two bellhops pushing luggage carts, a family with three jumping children, two teenage girls on cell phones with bags full of Fifth Avenue shopping. *Why would anyone want to travel to New York in the winter?* I thought. And then I realized, that could have been us.

I hit the UP button on one side of the elevator bank. Matty jiggled the UP button on the other side. I wanted to tell him to stop, but he was nervous, and getting it out. I was nervous, and telling him to stop would be me letting it out.

I breathed. I let the flow of air come through my nose, and I let the smooth fluid movement calm me.

I glanced behind my shoulder at Matty. Velma and Matty huddled close, ready to make our final good-byes and see me off into the battlefield.

We stood at the door, my bare knees knocking.

The elevator hit the second floor and continued to fall.

I glanced at Velma. She nodded, restrained. I could tell she was gearing up for it, as much adrenaline pounded through her body as mine. Even her black eye looked sober and ready.

The doors slid open.

"—put the explosives into storage," Preston was saying. "I mean, we could get rid of them, but you never know when you're going to be stuck in New York and need another batch . . . ."

He was still standing there, talking. The only other man in the elevator, a skinny, secretarial type with a curly horseshoe of disappearing hair, was busy scribbling down Preston's words.

I strode into the elevator.

In the background, Matty scurried away. Velma stepped into the elevator behind me and jammed the DOOR CLOSE button as I slammed my palm straight into the accountant's chest, cutting off enough blood to knock him out for a good hour.

I tossed the purse on top of the unconscious accountant. My credit card—that, I kept in my hand.

The elevator rushed upward. The air zoomed up fast, pressure building in my ears, much faster than elevators usually go. That was good; it meant that Matty had already hacked into the system—God knows from where—and he was in control. Preston clenched one fist around the security rail. The other went fishing for something in his pocket.

I put an end to that with one swift kick to his wrist.

Velma yelped and ducked into a corner.

Preston's cell phone tumbled from his hand. With his hand that still worked, he grasped the broken wrist. *"That HURT!"* he yelled. "I wasn't even going for a gun! What kind of monster *are* you, Candy?"

"I'm a monster," I said, stepping back from him, giving him space to feel the pain. "Now *that's* a joke."

"It wasn't supposed to be funny," he said, rubbing his wrist furiously. I rolled my eyes to the sky disbelievingly, but Velma was staring at him, taking in Preston's words from the corner that she was pressed into.

"You always think everything's about you, Candy. You, you, you. Why the hell would I chase you across all these cities? You think I don't have women hit on me every day of the year? You think you're that special?"

I watched him speak, confused. "You mean—you weren't sending those men to kill me?"

"To kill you?" Preston said, looking like he was about to laugh. "No way—"

—then the punch came, quick, straight into my face—

"They were just to mess with you." He smirked, lifting his fist into the air, pulling it back for another round. "The killing part, *that* was supposed to be all mine."

I doubled over in pain. Red leaked from my nose, tumbling down over my hands, making them sticky. The human nose is one of those places on your body that bleeds freely, and the damage always looks worse than it is. As a student of medicine, I knew that much.

But as a person, seeing that much blood spillage freaked me out. In spite of myself, I was trembling. I grabbed at my nose with both hands.

My credit card swished across the floor, past Velma's outstretched hand, and ricocheted off the wall.

I gave a little scream.

"What's wrong, princess?" Preston said, throwing me back against the far wall. "You were planning on murdering me with *that*?"

He pinned both my hands to the wall with his good hand. Beneath me was Velma, shrieking.

"You just wait till we get to the top floor," he crooned, leaning closer to me. His breath was on my face, now, heating my cheek, almost touching the spots of blood drying on my skin. The gravity from the rushing elevator beat both of us down, and we leaned on the walls to maintain our balance. "I have a hundred men waiting. I'll feed you to them, if I don't kill you first."

If I could regain my balance, I could kick him.

If I could break my hands free, I could punch him.

If he wasn't holding my arms so close, I could hit him with my head.

It's one of those things you do when you know martial arts. Running through limbs, positions, schools, and techniques, figuring out what you *could* do and what you *should* do. The better your enemy knows you, the better you can surprise him.

And the elevator was about to hit the top floor.

Preston shook. I shook. We both held tight to the corner of the elevator that we were pressed into, bracing ourselves against the walls for stability. His grip on my hands never loosened. I hooked one knee into the security handrail, getting ready to swing my other leg straight into his neck.

I wondered if I could collapse his Adam's apple.

The elevator slammed into the ceiling. There was a huge, dull *thud*, and the cabin shook. We all braced against the handrails as our bodies crashed into the walls. Then there was a smaller, sharp sudden gunpowder *crack*.

That was unexpected.

Preston and I looked up immediately, instinctively, wondering what would happen to the ceiling when we smashed.

Only I looked back down.

Preston's body trembled, wobbled, and fell.

It cascaded down slowly, jerkily, as if he were a puppet and someone had cut the strings. His arms fell. His knees dropped. His neck snapped down, and that handsome curly hair, textured with more processing lotions and expensive shampoos than the average teenage girl's head has seen in its lifetime, curled over his forehead and his eyes, like a curtain coming down at the end of a play.

Blood seeped through his shirt.

Preston collapsed against the far wall of the elevator, and shakily, I sank into the corner, breathing, clutching my chest, trying not to hyperventilate.

"Do you mind?" said Velma, squirming underneath me. "As much as you'd like to think of me as a trusty sidekick, I am *not* going to be your Ottoman footrest."

Nervously, I jumped up. I'd forgotten that she was even there.

"Oh no," Velma said, sliding the gun back into the pocket of her jeans. "Now we're going to have to deal with those hundred soldiers."

Her voice sounded hoarse, like she hadn't drank for days. Or like she'd been crying.

Only, Velma had never looked so sober.

From her other jeans pocket, she whisked out her cell phone and hit SEND. "Okay, Matty," she said. "I think you can open the doors now."

There was a moment's hesitation.

And the doors slid open.

Preston wasn't lying. We stepped into the corridor, and the hallway was filled with burly Neanderthals in Prada sunglasses and Valentino suits.

I fingered my credit card, which I'd snatched up off the floor in the aftermath of the gunshot. I sank into takeoff position for the spinning dragon.

Velma, hands resting on the wide girth of her hips, stepped across the bronze barrier of the elevator. She drew herself up to her full height, which was still, like, two-thirds of the way up to the average hit man's shoulder. She glared fiercely up at their faces.

Unnerved, the hit men stepped back, giving her a semicircle to step into.

"NOW LISTEN UP, YOU JERKS!" she yelled. "MY BEST FRIEND IS SICK AND TIRED OF YOU OAFS HUNTING HER! AND, TO BE QUITE HONEST, I'M GETTING A LITTLE BIT TIRED OF IT, TOO! YOUR LEADER'S DEAD IN THE ELEVATOR AND YOU'RE NOT LIKELY TO GET ANY MORE PAYCHECKS FROM HIM, SO IF YOU KNOW WHAT'S BEST FOR YOU, I SUGGEST YOU TURN AROUND AND GO TO YOUR PATHETIC LITTLE HOMES AND MICROWAVE YOURSELVES A GOOD SOLID DINNER, 'CAUSE I AM SICK OF THIS! OTHERWISE, I WILL STAND HERE AND TAKE OUT EACH OF YOU BY MYSELF! YOU GOT THAT?"

Dumb-faced, the crowd slowly filed into the elevator.

As if on cue, the other five elevators in the bank all slid open. The downward arrow lit up, and, in unison, they all gave a little *ding*.

"That was a nice touch at the end," Velma said to me, her voice even hoarser than it was before. "Matty's a good kid. I knew I didn't make him my just-friend for nothing."

With the rest of my body aching, sore, and fully uncooperative, I kissed the side of her head. "You were great, Velms," I said. "If people got awards for battles, you'd bring home an Oscar tonight."

I was smiling, but when Velma turned her head to look at me, her eyes were baggy and worn, a depth of sadness that I'd never seen in her before. It was almost like she wasn't capable of that kind of sadness, not sweet, perky Velma.

"I killed a man," she whispered. She spoke in the tiniest voice possible, but the hoarseness in her throat still crept through, and I recognized, not that cried-out feeling that I'd thought, but an even darker hoarseness of holding back tears, of someone who had not yet begun to cry.

"You saved my life," I offered weakly.

"That makes it better," she said. "But it doesn't make it right."

The elevators had mostly reached the bottom. One of them careened right back up, and the doors popped open. In it stood Matty, his laptop computer tucked under one arm. He looked really excited and a little bit perplexed.

"They left," he said. "All of them. I saw them leave. The biggest one even tousled my hair when he walked by, and he said something dumb. Like, 'Good luck in school, kid,' or something. I hate it when they call me 'kid.' I *really* hate it when they tousle my hair." He stopped, looked from Velma's face to mine and back again. "So it's really over?"

"Yes, Matty," I said. "It's really over."

"And we won?"

I looked at Velma.

"Well, we didn't lose," she said.

And then she reached up and tousled his hair.

We had to spend a bunch of time with the hotel clerks and the security people, explaining why the entire top two stories in the hotel were suddenly vacant and why one of their elevators was rickety, and then we had to spend even *more* time with the police, explaining everything else. Velma handled most of it, taking solace in jumping right into her normal role as hostess and clean-up girl, while I wandered over to the window, watching the people walk past and the snow fall on top of them, building up small piles of white on top of their coats and hats and scarves.

I felt someone coming up behind me, and then a hand on my shoulder.

It was Velma. "Come on," she said, "everything's taken care of."

"You mean, I don't have to offer a deposition or any of that stuff?"

"I *said*, it's taken care of."

I looked back and saw Mr. Patterson standing with his arm around the police commissioner, the two of them laughing innocently about some trivial matter.

"I don't have to, either?"

That was Matty. He was back to looking on top of the world, taking in everything, slick in his own bad fourteen-year-old way.

"No way," said Velma. "When I say it's over, it's over. You want to go celebrate or something?"

"Sure," Matty chirped up at once. "I know this great bar around here, it's where all the movie stars and models go. I'll bet they don't ID, and we can get beers and talk in loud voices about how cool we are . . . ."

"And that would be an ix-nay on the eer-bay for you, kiddo," Velma said, rustling his hair again. "Not to get all legal about it, but you've got to at least *look* twenty-one."

"See how long *you* last as a just-friend," Matty grumbled, kicking the floor.

At that point the police commissioner came up to us, with a bunch of officers and, just for good measure, Mr. Patterson. We made eye contact at once, and he grinned cheekily, but when the police commissioner started talking, we quickly switched to business mode.

"I think we've about wrapped up our investigation of what happened here tonight," he said. "With the tapes from the hotel surveillance cameras and the evidence in Reign's belongings, the facts are pretty self-explanatory. You shouldn't need to worry about testifying at all. You're very fortunate to have a friend in Mr. Patterson," he added, cupping Patterson's shoulder. "I'm just sorry you had to go through all this, ma'am."

And with that, they were gone, all the policemen and Mr. Patterson, and the night got a little quieter.

Then it was just the three of us, standing in the lobby like normal tourists.

"So this is the point where everything goes back to normal," said Matty.

"Not everything," Velma said, looking at me sadly. I knew she was thinking about my father.

But I was coming close to feeling dealable for about the first time in weeks, enough to walk around in public without sizing up every person in the room. And I sure wasn't going to spoil that with any hard-knocks whining.

"Life goes on," I said. "I just keep thinking, will I ever be able to catch up in class?"

And with that, Velma led us out of the hotel lobby, wrapping one of our arms in each of hers. We walked through the hotel's front entrance, and it slid open grandly, like the outside world was opening its doors to us.

All's Well That

Ends

(epilogue)

My cell phone rang in the middle of our epistemology review—the '80s electronic new wave ring, not the Motown one. Which meant it was my gold phone.

I shook myself out of that dazed sleepiness that review sessions always brought, the one where the outside world keeps broadcasting *just leave* through the windows and you know something bigger and better is going on outside the classroom walls.

I reached into my purse, grabbed the phone, and ran out of the room, ignoring all the hostile glares of my fellow students. All those nerds, the ones who I'd beat on the last three lab scores, stared at me, annoyed that I would think to answer my phone. Their beady eyes were like, *Geez—can't she even put her social life on hold for an exam?*

What they didn't know was, this call was anything but social.

I clicked the door shut behind me. The hallway was almost empty.

"Hey, baby," I said in a low whisper, ducking out of the hallway and into an empty classroom. "What have you got for me today?"

"No matter how low and sultry you talk, Candy Cohen, I am *not* going to turn straight."

"As if!" I cried, insulted. "I was ducking out of class!"

"That's what they all say," said Mr. Patterson in his gluey almost-British accent. "We just got a job request in, I'm thinking you're our girl. The pay is negotiable, but I'm sure it would cover the cost of next term's tuition."

I slouched against a blackboard and considered. "What's my backup?"

"Two dozen private security officers, Velma undercover, and that internet-savvy friend of yours, um, Matty, in charge of surveillance."

"Nice," I said. "Can we be done by midnight?"

"What's at midnight?"

"Just answer my question, Mr. Patterson."

"Sure, or else we'll pay time and a half."

"No—it's got to be *over*, kaput."

"You have my word." He clicked off.

So did I—and then I slipped back into class. The short hem of my lab coat brushed the even shorter hem of my miniskirt as I sat down.

After the job, the company helicopter flew us home. It soared over the city, dipped lower as it approached our section of town, and we hovered above the neighborhood cemetery for a second. Velma turned to me. "Do you want them to drop us off here?" she asked. In a much belated ceremony, we had finally interred my father.

"Nah," I said. "I'm not that sentimental."

The helicopter dropped down toward the roof of my apartment building. The old lady on the top floor peeked out the window in annoyance, but she always did. When we passed each other in the hall, she kept asking me if I heard the giant pigeons, too. I always agreed with her, just to make her feel better.

Tonight, I dropped my bags off in my room, splashed cold water on my face, and got out. I just grabbed my backpack and left.

Before I knew it, I was in my car, taking the highway at ninety miles an hour, tearing past wind and trees and drunken late-night motorists.

I didn't stop until I got to campus.

The grassy streets were all but deserted, a few students straggling home from bars and house parties like a dim recollection of the masses of kids that plow through the very same streets during the day.

I found my usual study carrel. It was on the third floor, in the back, piles of familiar-feeling textbooks stacked to the ceiling. I dug out my favorites, the vascular system and the human brain, and started studying.

The entire floor was empty, and nothing but aortas and veins echoed through my head. The night was warm, dingy, cozy in spite of the emptiness in the library. This hall was new. I could still smell the wood-work in the air.

A bronzed plaque, also brand new, had small-capital letters that weren't even dusty yet. If you read it, and not many people do, you'd see that the plaque commemorated this wing—the biological and medical wing of the library—TO DR. BENJAMIN COHEN, A LOCAL SURGEON, TAKEN FROM US BEFORE HIS TIME.

Velma had wanted the plaque to say that.

I told her, there's no such thing as before your time. Time, I realized, works in a lot of different ways. Some people spend their whole lives without taking five minutes to actually live. They may go to parties, schmooze with famous people—hell, they may have traveled the whole world and still not seen any of it.

But when you broke it down, time wasn't really like anything else. Even if I lived my whole life naturally, and died in bed at age one hundred and twenty from a broken record, I still wouldn't have enough time to learn everything I wanted to know, and do all the crazy things I wanted to do.

That's why I had to keep going.

Staying up late with a bio text—that was one thing. Nothing earth-shaking, but just something little that counted, that kept me happy. Reading about the breathing patterns of primates, climbing the genetic building blocks that will one day lead to working with actual humans. The only dancing I was doing tonight was with my numbers, watching bar graphs spiral off cliffs, kissing the pie charts of forever. In that abstract, unspoken way, it kind of felt like I was hanging out with my father when I got lost in these equations. Tomorrow, I could get shot through the heart. But at least I'd be able to say, I had a good last night. One damn good final night, with someone I care about.

Acknowledgments

by MATTHUE ROTH
edits by JODY CORBETT
produced by RICHARD NASH
designed by ANNE HOROWITZ
wardrobe BARUCH COHEN
hookups LUKE CARMODY
Czech editing MAREK JIRA
director of photography ITTA ROTH

Thanks to Itta, my partner in crime, cooking, and everything else, and to my parents, who support me no matter what mess I land in. Thanks to Alyssa, my sister, who taught me everything I know about chyck lit. And the crew: Jody, the best editor a kid could ask for. They don't pay her enough. Baruch Cohen, the book's fashion designer, who can outdress any supermodel any day of the week. Luke Carmody, director of hookups, and the first person who believed in a supermodel who could change the world. Marisa Castiginera, for her epic location scouting. Marek Jira, who makes me think I know Czech and doesn't tell anyone I don't. Writing this, my soundtrack was a mix of Jean Grae's Bootleg of the Bootleg E.P., Daphne Gottlieb's poems (yes, poems) and Kristen Kemp's The Dating Diaries. Thanks to

Burke, Justin Carlo, Cookie Jar & Onibi Vision, The End of the World, Katastrophe, Travis Morrison, Postal, Prowler, Edie Sedgwick, and Strand. Also, thanks to Rob, Bim, Ben, Hillel, Jen Joseph and Manic D Press for their advice; to Jonathan, Art, and Annalisa for gettin' my back; Javaman and the folks at Philtered.net; and to Anya, Fran, Aaron, and Dennis, for opening their kitchen and the rest of their house to me to write. To Rabbi Raz, Rabbi Davide, and the Brodts, for giving my soul a backbone and some ammo. And to Anne Horowitz and Jaime Rose Mendola.